VALLEY OF FEAR

Read all the Unicorns of Balinor books:

#1 The Road to Balinor
#2 Sunchaser's Quest
#3 Valley of Fear

Coming soon . . .

#4 By Fire, By Moonlight

UNICORNS OF BALINOR

VALLEY OF FEAR

MARY STANTON

AN
APPLE
PAPERBACK

SCHOLASTIC INC.
New York Toronto London Auckland Sydney
Mexico City New Delhi Hong Kong

Cover illustration by D. Craig

No part of this publication may be reproduced in whole or in part, or stored in a retrieval system, or transmitted in any form or by any means, electronic, mechanical, photocopying, recording, or otherwise, without written permission of the publisher. For information regarding permission, write to Scholastic Inc., Attention: Permissions Department, 555 Broadway, New York, NY 10012.

ISBN 0-439-06282-9

Text copyright © 1999 by Mary Stanton.
Illustrations © 1999 by Scholastic Inc.
All rights reserved. Published by Scholastic Inc.
SCHOLASTIC, APPLE PAPERBACKS, and associated logos are trademarks and/or registered trademarks of Scholastic Inc.

12 11 10 9 8 7 6 5   1 2 3 4/0

Printed in the U.S.A.   40
First Scholastic printing, July 1999

For
Julia Marie DiChario Clark,
and
Angela Nicole DiChario Clark
who believe in unicorns, too

VALLEY OF FEAR

1

Atalanta walked up the Eastern Ridge toward the cave of Numinor, the Golden One. She had grave news for him, and her steps were slow. The sun flooded mellow light across the top of the mountains surrounding the Celestial Valley. Atalanta's mane, tail, and horn glowed pale silver in the warm light. She was the Dreamspeaker, the Lady of the Moon, counselor to the unicorn herd of the Celestial Valley. The silver-white radiance was hers alone. The light of neither sun nor moon ever changed it.

Atalanta paused in her journey up the hill and looked down into the valley. The Celestial herd was settling in for the night. Each herd member was a different color of the rainbow. Their colors glowed like the dying embers of a campfire in the setting sun. Several gathered under the Crystal Arch, the long bridge that extended up to the cloud home of the One Who Rules and down to the humans' land of Balinor.

Atalanta's heart swelled with love at the sight of her home. The Celestial Valley, the Crystal Arch, and the unicorns themselves had been there for thousands of years. If she could only be sure that they would be there for thousands more!

Atalanta's forelock fell on either side of her crystal horn, shadowing her violet eyes. She paused, deep in thought. She was worried about Princess Arianna and her bonded unicorn, the Sunchaser. All had been well until the evil Shifter rose from his lair in the Valley of Fear to take over the throne of Balinor.

That had been a year ago. And for the unicorns and the people of Balinor, there had been nothing but grief and terror since the Shifter had kidnapped Arianna's parents, who were the rightful King and Queen. Arianna's brothers, the two young Princes, had also disappeared.

Atalanta had sent the High Princess and the Sunchaser beyond the Gap to safety at Glacier River Farm before the Shifter could get at them. The High Princess and her unicorn were the last hope of Balinor. Without them, there would be no way to bring the people and animals of Balinor together to overthrow the Shifter and his army.

Even as Atalanta approached the cave of Numinor, the Shifter hunted the Princess in Balinor.

Atalanta didn't know if Princess Arianna and her companions would make it back to Balinor Village from their recent journey. True, Tobiano, a Celestial Valley unicorn, was with Arianna and the Sunchaser as guardian and guide. And the human wizard Eliane Bohnes also accompanied them. But the Shifter could take any form — any form at all. How could Arianna and the Sunchaser fight an enemy they couldn't recognize? And the travelers were more than two days away from the village and safety.

Relative safety. Even the village of the Inn of the Unicorn, the home of the Resistance fighters against the Shifter and his army, had traitors among the thatched-roofed houses, spies on the cobblestone streets. No one was safe in these times.

Atalanta stood a moment longer. The sun set behind the Eastern Ridge and the last glow of sunlight faded. Atalanta raised her head and looked at the crescent moon riding low in the purple twilight. The Silver Traveler was faint and on the wane. Another week and she would be gone from the sky in her monthly journey around the earth. Then would come the time of the Shifter's Moon — which meant, of course, there would be no moon. A time when evil magic ruled, and the magic of Atalanta was at its lowest ebb.

The Shifter's Moon was no time for war. If there was ever a time for war. And Numinor would want to fight, once he heard what Arianna and the Sunchaser had to do now.

Atalanta shook herself and snorted gently into the twilight. She had to talk Numinor out of the impending war. If the Celestial unicorns were to attack the Shifter's forces, it had to be at a time and place when victory was possible. Arianna and the Sunchaser didn't have their full magical power, and that time wouldn't come soon.

Unless they accomplished the coming quest.

Atalanta resumed her journey up the hill.

The entrance to Numinor's cave was guarded by unicorns selected for their swiftness and courage. There were two sentries for each eight-hour shift. The two there this evening were from Atalanta's own color band of silver and white. They stood at attention in the courtyard, one at each of the two pillars that supported the entrance arch. The courtyard was paved with smooth, flat rock flecked with gold, which glittered in the low evening light.

Atalanta nodded to Ash, who guarded the left pillar, and spoke a word of greeting to Dusty, who guarded the right. Both sentries bowed deeply to her, forelegs to the ground, jeweled horns touching the pathway.

Atalanta walked across the courtyard, her silver hooves striking a barely audible chime. She heard the rhythmic pacing of Numinor in his cave, caught the now-bright, now-shadowy golden glow of his coat as he walked restlessly back and forth. She looked at Ash, then Dusty. "Would you leave us for a moment?"

The two faded obediently into the twilight.

Atalanta struck her horn gently against the pillar supporting the entrance arch. "Numinor!" she called. Her voice was low and sweet. In the depths of the cave, the sound of restless pacing stopped, and Numinor moved to the entrance. His coat was the gold of the sun at high noon. His horn was a shining spear. A deep yellow diamond — rarest of all jewels — glowed at the base of his horn.

Atalanta trotted forward. She gave Numinor the traditional formal greeting: They stood muzzle to muzzle for a brief minute, then she blew twice on his cheek. Her long silver mane swirled across his withers and mingled with the gold of his coat.

"Atalanta." Numinor's voice was deep and deceptively calm. Atalanta could smell the anger rising off him like a mist, could see anger in the sheen of sweat on the muscles of his great chest. He took a deep breath and rumbled, "You have news?"

"Yes." She backed away to see him better. Numinor's eyes were a rich mahogany-gold. She could see the angry pulse throbbing in the great vein at the side of his neck.

"The Sunchaser has his horn back," Numinor said abruptly. "The ruby jewel with his personal magic has been restored to the base. Now! *Now* we can attack! We will grind the Shifter to dust beneath our hooves! We will spear his army with our horns!"

"Now is *not* the time," Atalanta said, her own voice deliberately calm. "Let us stand and discuss this calmly."

"What is there to discuss, Atalanta? Now that the Sunchaser has his horn back, he and Princess Arianna are bonded again. The people and animals of Balinor won't lose the ability to speak to one another. And now they can work together to overthrow the Shifter. And we of the Celestial Valley will be there to help them — as we always have been."

"I wish it were that easy. Yes, the Sunchaser has his horn again. But this was just the first step, Numinor. You know the law of the One Who Rules Us All. Arianna and the Sunchaser are a Bonded Pair. They are the source of all bonds between humans and animals. Arianna is one half of that bonding. And she does not yet recall all of her past — she herself has not reclaimed her role as Princess."

"You must tell her, then. Help her remember."

Atalanta shook her head with a wry, regretful gesture. "I would have done that long before this if it would work. Explaining her past doesn't mean that her memories will be there. You know that, Numinor. You haven't forgotten what else was lost when

6

the Shifter attacked the Royal Family and destroyed the Sunchaser's horn."

"The Scepter!" Numinor's words rumbled and echoed around the cave. "The Royal Scepter!"

"Yes. Without *that*, the Princess will never remember all of who she is. Without the Scepter, the Sunchaser himself will not come into all of his magic. Arianna must find it. The power of the Princess and her Bonded unicorn are inextricably linked together."

Numinor ground his teeth, then bowed his head in acceptance. "What must be, must be." His whole body quivered with the need for action. "Where is the Scepter to be found?"

"It was torn from the Palace during the fight following the Great Betrayal."

"I know that," he said impatiently. "But do you know where it *is*, Atalanta?"

The Dreamspeaker nodded reluctantly. "We unicorns cannot rescue the Royal Scepter. We unicorns can't touch it or even help her get to it. It is Arianna's quest. She must go and find it."

"Where is it, then?!" Numinor struck out with one great foreleg. A gold flame leaped from the spot where his hoof hit the floor. "She must get it back. You can tell her where it is, at least."

"I am afraid to tell her."

"But why?"

"The Royal Scepter of Balinor," Atalanta said slowly, "lies across the Sixth Sea in the Valley of Fear, hidden in the Castle Entia." Her violet eyes clouded with tears. "It lies at the very heart of the Shifter's evil. No one who has ever gone to the Valley of Fear has ever come back —" She stopped, and the next word was so soft that Numinor barely heard it: "— alive."

2

"**I**'m homesick," Lori Carmichael said. "Homesick, homesick, *homesick!*" She and Arianna lay on their backs around the campfire, looking up at the crescent moon. Dr. Bohnes had disappeared into the night some time ago on a search for food to augment the meager rations they were carrying. They had left the Inn of Luckon to travel back to Balinor Village with as many provisions as they could carry in the unicorns' saddlebags but their supply was low.

Lori scowled angrily. Her blond hair was matted and her face was dirty. "We're stuck here in the cold and damp while we wait for food. Somebody didn't plan this very well, if you ask me."

No one answered her. The Sunchaser and Toby grazed nearby. Ari, her head propped up on a saddlebag, watched Chase through half-closed eyes. His ebony horn was almost invisible at night, but his bronze coat caught the gleam of firelight. It was amazing, the transformation that had come upon him with the restoration of his horn and the jewel at its base. The muscles of his chest were more sharply defined. He seemed taller. His mane rippled down his withers like a river of bronze water. His hooves were solid bronze that never chipped or cracked. A subtle light came from him — no matter what the time of day or night — so that he seemed to move in a pool of bronze starlight.

Chase raised his head and looked across the fire at her. She smiled at him.

Chase! she said with her thoughts.

Milady! he replied.

I miss Lincoln, she thought. *I'm anxious to see my dog again.*

Dr. Bohnes said he will be waiting to greet us when we get back to the village, Chase thought in answer. The unicorn dropped his head to the grass again and went on grazing.

"Didn't you hear me?" Lori demanded. The blond girl sat up abruptly, a scowl on her face. She pulled angrily at the twigs in her hair. "I said I want to go home. Back to Glacier River Farm. And I want to go now!"

"Yes," Arianna said, "I heard you." She sat up and rubbed her calf. They had been on the road three days since the battle to regain Chase's horn at the Palace, and her legs were hurting again. She rolled the left leg of her breeches up and pulled her sock off. The campfire didn't provide a lot of light, but she could see the scar spiraling down from her knee to her ankle. Why did her injury hurt so much, six months after the leg had been set? Wasn't she ever going to be free of the pain?

"I suppose you're going to tell me you can't talk because you're in *soooo* much pain," Lori snapped.

"That's more than enough," Tobiano said sternly. The black-and-white unicorn gave a short, angry snort through his horn. "You ought to be ashamed of yourself."

Lori had the grace to look embarrassed. "Sorry," she muttered. "I didn't mean that like it sounded."

"Her Royal Highness was lucky to survive the trip through the Gap to Glacier River Farm with just two broken legs," Toby continued, "and I don't re-call that Her Royal Highness extended a written in-vitation to you to come here to Balinor, did you, Your Highness? No, Lori, you just showed up here all by yourself. Driving Her Highness to distraction with your whining."

"It wasn't my fault," Lori said. She tried to look virtuous and only succeeded in looking bratty. "I fell through the Gap by accident. Who knew that your stupid magic was going to drag me through that tunnel into a place where horses with horns stuck on their heads do nothing but *yak, yak, yak* in my face all day long!"

Toby, who was short, stubby, and extremely

sensitive about the fact that he didn't have the elegance of his herdmates in the Celestial Valley, swelled up like a rooster. "I," he said, "am a *unicorn*. I am *not* a horse with a horn stuck on my head, you rude little girl."

"Toby," Ari began, "we only have a few more days on the road before we get back to the village. Please, let's —"

Toby snorted furiously. "Whine! Complain! Whine! Complain! That's all you ever do!"

"Be quiet!" Ari shouted.

Toby shut up like a clam about to be dropped in a stew pot.

"I'll vote for that," Lori grumbled.

Ari threw her blanket from her shoulders and rose stiffly to her feet. She didn't feel like a princess at all. She was tired, hungry, and she hadn't had a bath for three days. She rubbed her hands over her face, scrubbing at the grit of three days' travel. She wanted her dog. She wanted to be clean. She didn't want to face any more danger — especially if there would be danger to Chase or even to the horrid Lori. Ari still didn't remember much about her past as a Princess — but wasn't it supposed to be easier than this?

She put her hands on her hips and surveyed Lori with a sigh. "Homesick? I can understand you being homesick."

Lori stuck out her chin and turned her back. "Well? Don't *you* want to go home?" Her voice was thick with tears. "Don't you miss your foster parents?"

"You miss your mom and dad, don't you?" Ari thought about Lori's father, who was red-faced and loud. Her hand went to the knife in the scabbard at her belt. Mr. Samlett, the Innkeeper at Balinor Village, had said the knife belonged to her own father. The King. The King of Balinor.

Why couldn't she remember him more clearly? She had flashes of memory: a huge man, with a blond beard and a laugh to shake the ceiling. And her mother, the Queen: quiet and fragrant with the scent of roses around her like a cloak. But she couldn't remember any more, no matter how hard she tried. Why did all her memories drift like fragments of cloud across the sun?

A soft chime, like a silver bell, sounded in the depths of the woods behind her. Sunchaser lifted his head, eyes wide and dark, and stared off into the trees.

Lori flung herself onto a log near the campfire. She clearly hadn't heard the quiet ringing. "I guess you want to stay here in Balinor, since everyone here believes you are their long-lost Princess."

"I don't feel like their long-lost Princess. I don't *want* to be their long-lost Princess." Ari was scared. She was afraid of the Shifter, afraid of the trouble being the Princess would cause her friends.

What if she just couldn't do it? What if she

13

just stood up, announced that she wanted the normal life of a normal thirteen-year-old, and took Chase and went off to be herself?

She avoided looking over at Chase. Dr. Bohnes and the Dreamspeaker, Atalanta, had told her that Chase was now Lord of the Animals in Balinor. Or would be, as soon as she assumed her rightful place on the throne. Would he want an ordinary life? What was his rightful place?

Ari scrubbed at the ground with her worn sandal. They'd been wearing nice, ordinary riding breeches and boots when magic flung them through the Gap. Now Ari wore a long red skirt, a soft muslin blouse, and a leather vest that Dr. Bohnes called a jerkin. One of the leather straps on her rough sandals had come loose. It dragged in the dust as she scraped her sandal back and forth.

Lori watched her for a long moment, then asked, "If you don't feel like a Princess, what *do* you feel like, then?"

"Lost," Ari said slowly. "I feel lost. It's a terrible thing when your memory comes and goes like summer rainstorms. They tell me I'm the Princess. I remember just a few things about being Princess. Something of the Palace before the Shifter's forces took over. My father's face. My mother's presence. But all I really know, Lori, is that Chase is mine. Chase will always be mine. Everything else . . ." She shrugged. "It's as if it happened to someone else.

And I don't feel homesick because I don't know where my home is."

The bell-like chime called again. Lori was oblivious to the sound. Ari listened, holding her breath so that she could hear even the slightest whisper. She looked at Chase. His head was up, his eyes eager. So! He had heard it, too. She looked at Toby. Stout little Toby, rude and belligerent and a little comic.

But at the moment, Toby didn't look comic at all. He looked stern, and a little frightening. He stared at her, his brown eyes commanding her to go.

The bell sounded a third time.

Third and last.

"I have to go," Ari said.

"Go? Go where?" Lori asked crossly. She darted a glance at the trees surrounding them, then she whirled and glared at Ari. "Into the woods? Are you crazy? This . . . this Shifter person is all around here, or so that crazy old veterinarian said."

"Dr. Bohnes is not a crazy old anything," Ari said evenly. She took one step toward the woods, then another. What was calling her? She looked at Chase.

You must go alone, he thought at her. *I will come if you need me.*

"But . . . what is it?" Ari whispered.

Chase said nothing, but gazed at her with his deep, dark eyes. Lori, unconscious of anything but her own grievances, chattered on, "All right, all right. So, Dr. Bohnes says she was your old nurse here in Balinor or whatever. But Ari, back at Glacier River — back *home* — she was the vet at your farm." Her eyes followed Ari as the bronze-haired girl moved slowly toward the woods. Lori's voice rose and she spoke faster and faster. "And who knows what she really is, this Dr. Bohnes? Who knows what *anyone* really is in this crazy place. . . . Ari! Come back here! Don't you dare leave me alone with this talking horse!"

"Unicorn," Toby said, his tone unexpectedly deep. "Let Her Royal Highness go, Lori Carmichael. This is no business of yours."

Ari stepped out from the comforting glow of the fire and into the woods. The pale light of the crescent moon didn't penetrate here. She stood a moment until her eyes adjusted to the dark. There was the rustle of a small creature in the brush, the faint scent of damp leaves, the strong odor of pine needles.

Ari cleared her throat and said, "Um . . . hello?"

A shadow shifted to her left. Ari grasped the knife at her side, willing herself to stand still. "It's Ari — I mean, Arianna," she said aloud. "Did . . . did someone call me?"

Silence. She began to wonder if she'd imagined the crystalline chime of the bell. And then, deep in the woods, a lavender-blue light began to glow. The light was soft at first, and dim. Ari walked toward it, careful not to scuff the leaves in her path, careful to move as quietly as she could.

A breeze lifted the leaves in the trees, and a scent of flowers came to her, a scent she had smelled before. Her heart began to beat faster. She recognized that blue-white radiance — didn't she? And that smell of flowers that never grew upon this earth . . . that was familiar, too.

She crept toward the light, which was growing steadily stronger now, until it illuminated the very tops of the trees. The source was — where?

There. At the foot of the tallest oak in the forest, or so it seemed to Ari. A faint sound of trickling water came to her. She stopped and shaded her eyes with her hand.

The most beautiful unicorn stood beneath the oak. Her coat was a milky silver shadowed with violet light. Her mane swept in a long fall to her knees. Her head was bent, so that Ari couldn't see her eyes, and her crystal horn just touched the surface of the water in a small stream trickling past her hooves.

"Atalanta," Ari breathed.

The Dreamspeaker raised her head. Her deep violet eyes smiled. She nodded once and then spoke, her voice as gentle as the fall of petals.

"Come here, child."

17

"The Lady of the Moon," Ari said. "They call you the Dreamspeaker. You rescued me from the mob at the Inn. The mob led by Lady Kylie."

"Come closer, Arianna, and sit here at my feet. You must learn your fate."

3

"Sit down, my child," Atalanta said.

Shyly, Ari curled herself at the unicorn's feet. Surrounded by the Dreamspeaker's magical radiance, her doubts and fears ebbed away. "I missed you," she said. "I wish you could be near me always."

"I am here now." Atalanta settled gracefully onto the forest floor, hindquarters tucked under herself. Her forelegs curved around Ari's back. Ari settled into the silky warmth of the unicorn's side and twined her hand in Atalanta's silver mane. "Now tell me, Arianna. What is troubling you?"

Ari looked deep into Atalanta's violet eyes. There could be no holding back in her response. Those purple eyes could see lies and evasions and half-truths. "I don't want to be the Princess!" she said. "Part of me knows that being the Princess means giving up things. I will always have to think of others first. I'll have to *do* things for others before I do things for myself. I won't have a life of my own!"

"That is true," the Dreamspeaker said calmly. "But there are great rewards in fulfilling your destiny, Arianna. There is both peace and love within you, my child. Those feelings, those qualities will come to full flower when you work for the benefit of your people."

"What if I can't?" Ari asked. "What if . . . what if I become cruel and selfish?"

"What will be, will be, Arianna. We all feel cruel and selfish at times. Greedy. Angry. Spiteful. But you have a choice, don't you? You aren't at the mercy of your feelings. You also have a brain and a heart. You can decide for yourself. You have been afraid before."

"Petrified," Ari agreed.

"You conquered the fear. You made a choice to be brave. And you succeeded. You have another choice now. Can you bear what I am about to tell you? And can you make the right choice this time, too?"

"I don't know if I can," Ari said humbly. "I'm awfully scared."

"You'd be a fool not to be frightened, Arianna. And you are not a fool. True bravery, genuine courage, comes from enlightened fear. Do you understand me?"

"I think so," Ari said. "It's easier not to know if something's going to be truly bad. But I'm not as scared when you're here. This — whatever it is that I'm going to have to do now — can you come with me?"

"No."

"No? Just no?"

Atalanta's eyes seemed to smile, but her gentle voice was firm. "I am the Dreamspeaker. You are the Princess of Balinor. It is not within my power to do other than I am doing now. I am a guide, Arianna, a counselor. I cannot be other than I am. Tell me, do you wish to return to Glacier River Farm?"

"Do you mean — I could?"

Atalanta nodded slightly. "Yes. You could."

"But . . . my parents. Who will find them if I don't?"

"There are those in the Resistance who will try."

"Will they rescue them? Find my father and make him King again? Find my mother and my brothers?"

"Perhaps. Perhaps not."

"Chase and I would have a better chance to find them?"

"Yes. It is what you were born to do. But first, there is one task you must complete. *If* you can do it. If you can go on this quest and return in triumph, then the people of Balinor will rally around you and the Sunchaser. And there is good reason for that, Arianna. You and the Sunchaser have a hereditary magic that is given to no others in the kingdom. This

21

is why the Shifter is afraid of you. Why he and his army of phantom unicorns are looking for you even now. But yes, if you wish to return to Glacier River, to cross the Gap to safety, I can contrive to send you both back. But Chase must give up his horn and his personal magic. And you must renounce your claim to the throne. Forever."

"I would be an ordinary girl," Ari said. "I think I might be better as an ordinary girl than as a Princess, Dreamspeaker. Trying to remember what it was like to be a Princess is like trying to grab water. The memories spill right out of my mind. And I feel silly when people curtsy to me. I'm embarrassed when everyone calls me 'Royal Highness.' I don't feel very royal."

"I see."

"Could I be an ordinary girl?"

"It is your choice, Arianna. Anale and Franc would continue to be your foster parents. You could live at Glacier River Farm and go to school there. You could train horses. Teach the young on that side of the Gap to ride. Perhaps" — Atalanta's tone was thoughtful — "perhaps tell them tales of legendary unicorns."

For a moment, Ari lost herself in a safe and reassuring dream. Her memories of Glacier River Farm were clear, distinct, and recent. She remembered the green meadows, the gray barns and white fences. And the horses — nice, ordinary horses named Cinnamon and Scooter and Duchess. She could go to school, make friends with other ordinary girls.

And the Sunchaser, too, would be an ordinary horse. And perhaps, at night, dream of the life he was meant to lead. Lord of the Animals here in Balinor.

She couldn't do that to Chase. She couldn't change his destiny. Or her own.

Ari sighed. "Well," she said. "I guess not. I suppose I'd better do what I have to do."

"You are certain?"

"No. I'm not certain. I'm scared. But I'll do it. Whatever it is, I'll do it. You're sure you can't come with me?"

Atalanta shook her head. Her mane swept over Ari's cheek.

"So Chase and I will be all alone?"

"Not quite alone. There are four who will travel with you and the Sunchaser. You will be the Company of Six." She was silent, and then said with an odd hesitation in her voice, "I believe there is one other who will help you. But I am not certain of this. She is part of the deep magic. You must seek advice from the Old Mare of the Mountain."

The words sent a strange thrill through Arianna. Her breath caught in her throat. "Who — who is that?"

Atalanta closed her eyes for a long moment. "I cannot tell you more. Not now." Her long lashes swept up, and her deep violet eyes held Ari's. "This is a great task you are asked to do, Arianna. Some of it involves the deep magic. I have not been permitted to see all. That will be revealed to you in time — I have seen this in the Watching Pool, and what is in the pool is true. I can only hope that the four who travel with you and Chase will have magic of their own. I can only hope that you will see the Old Mare. But, just in case of trouble that I have not foreseen, I am permitted to give you this. To use only in time of your greatest need." Atalanta dipped her horn into the stream, then tossed her head. The sparking water whirled in a tiny vortex around the tip of her horn, then coalesced into a starry point. "Hold out your hand, my child."

Obediently, Ari held her hand out. The starry tip of Atalanta's horn fell into her open palm. Ari looked at it, fascinated. The tip had formed into a small flask filled with diamond-clear water. She closed her hand around it. It was cool, as cool and chilly as rain.

"This is the Star Bottle. Use it only when all is dark and there seems no hope. This — and your own courage, Arianna — should be enough. With these, you will not be alone." She nuzzled Ari's hair gently, the breath from her muzzle soft and fragrant. "You must ask me, child, what this great task will be. I will wait until you are ready."

Ari swallowed tears of fright. She snuggled into Atalanta's side. If only she didn't have to be the

Princess! If only she could lie here with the Dream-speaker, safe and content forever!

The unicorn lay quietly with her, the soft sounds of her breathing as comforting as the sounds of waves at the seashore. Finally Ari said, too loudly, "Please, tell me."

"You must find the Royal Scepter. Do you remember it?"

Ari stared straight ahead, concentrating. "I think so. It's not very big, is it? About the size of a riding crop."

"It is made of rosewood and set with lapis lazuli."

"And there's a carved unicorn's head on the top."

"Yes."

Ari focused as hard as she could on the elusive memory. The Scepter had special powers — she remembered that, at least. "Chase!" she exclaimed. "The Scepter is a visible token of my bond with Chase! It was passed to me when we bonded."

"When you find it, you will come into all your powers as High Princess. Your memories will return to you. All of them. You and the Sunchaser will have full use of the Bonded Magic." The silver light around Atalanta began to dim. Ari tightened her hold on the unicorn's mane. "What's happening?" she cried.

"I must return to the Celestial Valley," Atalanta

said. The light was fading faster now. "The Scepter is in the power of the Shifter, Arianna. You and the Sunchaser must return to Balinor Village and prepare for a two-week journey to his home in the Valley of Fear. You must travel in disguise all the way, for the Shifter's spies are everywhere."

"Disguise?" Ari asked.

"When you journey through Balinor and the lands beyond, you will go as ordinary citizens of Balinor. As soon as you reach the Valley of Fear, you must appear to be soldiers of the Shifter's army."

"So there will be no battle," Ari said. She relaxed a little. This sounded possible. "Do we walk to the Valley of Fear then?"

"Samlett will take you in the cart to Sixton, a village on the shore of the Sixth Sea. There you will ask for Captain Tredwell, of the ship named the *Dawnwalker*. He will equip you with the soldier's disguise — he's been to many strange places, Captain Tredwell! And he will take you to the Valley of Fear."

"The . . . the . . . home of the Shifter," Ari faltered.

"Yes, Arianna." Atalanta got to her feet. Ari rose with her, and released her tight hold on the unicorn's mane. "His true home. Where his true form lies. The being who occupies your own Palace is only a shadow of his evil. Not the evil itself."

Ari's mind was whirling. "Can Chase and I do this?"

"The Sunchaser has known for some time about the Valley of Fear. And of the need to find the Royal Scepter."

"He never said anything to me."

"He knows — as I do — that the decision rests with you."

Ari didn't know anything about the Valley of Fear. And she was pretty sure she didn't want to know. The ghouls who guarded her own Palace now that the Shifter had taken the throne of Balinor were horrible — not even human. She supposed that the Valley of Fear was filled with ghouls worse than those she and Chase had just fought.

"Yes," Atalanta said, as if reading her thoughts. "The Shifter's army came from the Valley of Fear before they occupied Balinor. There is still a garrison there. But you will have as much help as Numinor and I can give you.

"First, I have spoken to Numinor. We will create a diversion as soon as you reach Sixton. A band of Celestial unicorns will walk the Path from the Moon to Balinor for the first time in our history. We will appear on the grounds of the Palace in Luckon, and we will lead the Shifter on a merry chase."

"You won't fight?" Ari asked. "You're sure?"

"We are not ready," Atalanta said simply. "Although Numinor is quite angry about it. We cannot fight until you and Chase are a fully Bonded Pair again. While we are leading the Shifter and his soldiers away from the Palace, you and your five com-

27

panions will enter Castle Entia and reclaim the Scepter." Atalanta's light was almost gone. Ari could barely see her in the dark, just the crystal horn, which glowed with blue-white light. "You must enter the Valley of Fear. Follow the lava path to the Castle Entia itself. Take no food or water into that place. The Scepter lies concealed beneath one of the Shifter's greatest victories."

"One of his greatest victories?" Ari asked, bewildered. "What is that?"

But only the glow was left. Atalanta herself was gone.

There was no answer. Just the gentle spill of water over rocks in the stream. And then the trickling water stopped, and there was no sound at all.

Great grief and fear welled up in Ari's heart. The feelings were so strong, tears came to her eyes. She bit her lip, hard, and then she coughed to keep from crying. She tucked the Star Bottle into her scabbard, next to her father's knife.

She went back to the campfire, and to Chase. There was so much yet to be done.

4

"**W**here have you *been*?!" Lori shrieked as Ari walked out of the woods and into the warmth surrounding the campfire. "I've been all by myself here!" Lori wrapped her arms around her chest and shivered. "The fire's going out."

"I told her to get more wood," Toby said.

"*You* get more wood," Lori said angrily. "What am I, your slave?"

Toby's affronted expression was such a perfect example of "What? The great *me*?" that Ari had to laugh.

"What's so funny?" Lori scowled.

"Why don't we all gather some wood," Ari said diplomatically. "I'll take Chase and you take Toby, and we'll pick up enough to last the rest of the night."

"I don't want to," Lori sulked. "There are *things* out there in the woods."

"True enough. But if we go together we'll be safe, I think. I have my knife, and Chase and Toby have their horns."

"Listen! Just listen! Can't you hear that horrible howling?"

One long, mournful cry split the night. Then came another howl. Chase lifted his head. His ears swiveled forward. He whinnied a challenge. A chorus of howls came in response. Despite herself, Ari shivered.

"Wolves," Lori said, with the sort of satisfaction people get when the worst has been confirmed. "A pack of them."

"Dr. Bohnes isn't back yet," Ari said with concern. "And she should have returned by now." The chorus of howls cut off, and then there was a yelp. Ari set her mouth in a firm line. "Forget the firewood. We'd better set out and look for Dr. Bohnes."

"No need," Chase said. "She's almost here."

Chase's ears were keener than those of humans. It was some minutes before Ari heard the steady tromp of Dr. Bohnes. The tough little vet stamped out of the bushes and came toward them. She had a load of firewood on her back, and she clutched a large bag against her chest. Her white hair was damp with sweat.

"Oh, Dr. Bohnes!" Ari cried. She ran forward and grasped the bundle of firewood. "Stand still a second, so I can take this off your shoulders." She lifted the bundle off the doctor's shoulders, and Dr.

Bohnes sat down suddenly. "You should have taken Toby with you," Ari scolded gently.

"It's not heavy," Dr. Bohnes gasped. "Just got a little winded coming up the rise. I had help most of —"

Suddenly, Lori pointed a trembling finger behind Dr. Bohnes and shrieked.

"— the way," Dr. Bohnes finished. She glowered at Lori. "Hush, now. They don't like screaming. Hurts their ears."

"Hurts *whose* ears . . . oh!" Ari said. Three long shadows slunk into the light of the dying fire.

"Wolves," Toby said. "Phuut!" He lowered his horn menacingly.

"Stop!" Dr. Bohnes commanded him. She held out her hand. "Rufus. Tige. Sandy. Come and meet Arianna and the Sunchaser."

The wolf in the lead was larger than his two fellows. All three had thick gray coats, freckled with rust and white. The tip of the leader's tail was reddish brown. They moved cautiously, heads low to the ground, sharp teeth visible in wolfish grins. The wolf with the red-brown tail looked up at Dr. Bohnes. His eyes were yellow, with round black pupils constricted to pinpoints by the firelight. Dr. Bohnes nudged his thick fur with her toe. She beamed affectionately at him. "Good old Rufus," she said.

"May we see them?" His voice was mellow and slow.

"Arianna! Stand up straight, girl. This is Rufus, leader of the Forest Pack. Rufus and Tige, this is Her Royal Highness, Arianna, Princess of Balinor." Dr. Bohnes dropped the sack she was carrying with a thud. The third wolf howled mournfully. "And Sandy, too. Sorry, Sandy. Anyway, I promised them they could have a look at you and Chase. They've been loyal supporters of the Crown, of course."

"Um," Ari said. "Uh . . . welcome." This didn't seem very princesslike. And now, because she was committed to her fate, she might as well try being a little more — impressive.

But she didn't feel very impressive. Her skirt was grubby and spotted with sticker-burrs. Her blouse had a big grass stain on it. And her hair was a mess. She stood up a little straighter and deepened her voice. "Welcome, loyal subjects of the Crown." She ignored Lori's giggle with what she hoped was Royal dignity.

"And there!" the wolf behind Rufus whispered in excitement. He gazed, quivering, at the Sunchaser. "Your Majesty!" All three wolves dropped to the ground, then rolled over, exposing their tawny bellies. They lay with their forepaws in the air, gazing adoringly — upside down — at Chase. Ari bit back a giggle. This was exactly the way dogs behaved.

Chase, Ari admitted to herself as she watched, really knew how to handle the Royal dignity part of being Lord of the Animals. He stood proudly, confident but without arrogance. Every muscle in his great body was defined under his glistening bronze coat. The ruby jewel at the base of his horn gleamed like a banked coal in an inviting fire. His ebony horn shone.

"Your Majesty!" Rufus said. "A word!"

"Please come forward." Chase had just the right combination of wisdom, majesty, and kindliness in his voice. Ari smiled at him. He half-lowered one eyelid in a mischievous wink. Rufus rolled over onto his feet. Head low, tail wagging gently, he walked toward the Sunchaser. Rufus had his own kind of dignity, Ari noted. He was respectful without being servile. He had the right kind of pride, too: pride in himself and his kind, without being aggressive. Sandy and Tige followed two strides behind their pack leader. The two of them waited until Rufus stood directly in front of the Sunchaser.

"You may sit," Chase said.

Rufus sat first, forepaws together, ears up, eyes leveled at Chase's chest. Sandy and Tige took their places on either side of Rufus. They lay on the ground and looked into the distance. Ari realized that this posture signaled obedience to the Sunchaser's will.

"You have been absent too long, Your Majesty." There was regret — and something else — in Rufus's speech. He was worried. That was it, Ari decided. The pack leader was concerned.

"I *have* been away too long," Chase agreed.

"And I may be absent yet awhile, wolf. My full powers have not been returned to me. There is . . ." He turned his dark eye on Ari. Atalanta was right. Chase knew about the Valley of Fear. He knew what Atalanta needed her to do. He knew about the quest. ". . . a task before me that will take me once again away from Balinor."

"For how long, sire?"

"A month. From Shifter's Moon to Shifter's Moon."

Sandy and Tige howled softly. Rufus lowered his head, panted, and then looked up. "We have trouble, Your Majesty. In the forest."

Chase waited patiently.

"You know that we were losing our way of speech with the humans of Balinor. More than speech left us, Your Majesty. We — that is, many of us — became wordless. And with the loss of words came something else. The loss of our selves. We held fewer and fewer Councils. Those that we did hold became places of great danger. Some of us — some of my own pack, Your Majesty — began to prey on others."

The wrinkles over Chase's eyes deepened.

"Yes, sire. We eat insects, grubs, nuts, berries, and fruits. But as our words left us, so did our appetite for eating these safe things."

"And?"

Rufus dropped his head to his paws, then

raised it. "There is now a hunt. For rabbit. Deer. For small creatures, such as mice."

A shudder passed through Chase's frame. His mind screamed, but no audible sound passed from him, so only Ari heard. She bit her lip to keep from screaming herself.

"The wolves only?" Chase asked, after a long moment.

"Ah. I thought perhaps the others would tell you of their crimes, sire. I only speak for my pack. I do not bear tales of others' crimes."

"My good wolf," Chase commanded. "Who commits the hunt? And when? Tell me!"

Tell me, Ari echoed silently.

Rufus turned around several times in agitation, following his tail with a fierce intensity. At last he settled on his haunches, facing his King. "The big cats, as well as my pack. The bears. The ferrets. The great birds. Thank the One Who Rules that dragons have all but disappeared from Balinor."

"Be still," Chase said, cutting him off. "Enough." He lowered his head. He scraped one foreleg across the earth. "And now? The animals of Balinor have had their words restored to them, Rufus, with the return of my horn. Her Royal Highness and I do not have command of our full magic, but speech between animal and human, at least, has been saved. There is no excuse to break the law. Does the hunt continue?"

"It does, Your Majesty. To my sorrow. There are those who now have a taste for . . . for blood."

"Those who hunt," Ari asked, "have they renounced their King? Have they turned to the Shifter as their monarch?"

Rufus turned his head to Sandy. He touched the other wolf with his forepaw, then nodded to him. "Tell them," he said. "Tell the King."

Sandy threw back his head and howled, a long, agonizing cry that took Ari's breath away. "Yes, Your Highness," Sandy said. "And my own brother Fig is among them."

All three wolves howled in grief. Ari felt the back of her neck prickle.

"Well, honestly," Lori said. "This is stupid. It's the way things are. I mean, I'm sorry, but that's what the world's like. Big fish eat little fish. Little fish eat teeny fish."

"Not here," Chase said.

"But —"

He whirled, then reared, his horn piercing the night. "NOT HERE IN BALINOR!" He came to all fours with a crash. Lori, her face pale, sat down with a thump.

Rufus broke the long silence. "There is a Council of the Animals called for the last night of the crescent moon, Your Majesty. Will you come?"

Chase turned to Ari. "I must," he said. "It will add two days to our journey home. But I must be there."

36

Ari nodded. "We will come to the Council, Rufus. Where shall we meet?"

The wolf looked at her with his yellow eyes, then squeezed them open and shut, open and shut. "Thank you, Your Highness. Thank you. We meet at the red oak, by Staines Waterfall."

"We shall see you there, then, pack leader." Chase blew out with a long, angry whistle. "And take this message to all who live in the forest. The law has been broken. Those who broke the law will be judged. And sentence will be passed."

The wolves dropped to their bellies to signify obedience. Then they melted off into the night.

Dr. Bohnes cleared her throat, then began to feed the fire with the wood she'd brought back. Ari opened the sack of provisions that Dr. Bohnes had dropped on the ground, and methodically laid out wheat cakes, apples, and cheese. She set aside a canister of oats meant for Toby and Chase.

"Hel-*lo-oh*," Lori said in a very sarcastic way. "Isn't anybody going to say anything?"

"What is there to say?" Ari set half of the oats in front of Toby, and took the other half to Chase. She handed Dr. Bohnes a thick slice of bread, an apple, and a ball of goat cheese.

"So we're going to add two extra days to this stupid trip."

"We must," Ari said.

"We *must*," Lori mimicked furiously. "What we *must* do is start figuring out a way to get back to

37

Glacier River. Let these guys figure out for themselves what to do."

"We can't, and that's final, missy," Toby said. "Eat your cheese. And if you're not going to eat that apple, give it to me."

"Get your own apple, Toby," Lori said. She bit into her apple with a loud crunch. "Ari, this hunt is not our problem."

Toby shook his head violently. "It most certainly is our problem." He began to eat his oats. Grain spilled out of the sides of his muzzle. "Animals who hunt deer and rabbit aren't going to stop at that for dinner." He paused, head up, listening. The howls of the departing wolf pack floated across the crescent moon. "I want to be sure those howls are friendly. That they aren't the sound of the Shifter's pack hunting . . ." He swallowed his oats with a gulp.

"Hunting what?" Lori asked.

Toby blinked at her. "Hunting us."

5

"**O**f course I'm going with you to the Council," Dr. Bohnes said. "Don't be ridiculous. You need me."

Ari had spent a restless night, lying back-to-back with Chase near the fire. She had dreamed fitfully. Not the sort of dreams sent by Atalanta, but horror-filled nightmares. Eagles darted at her out of a flaming sky, beaks wide and hungry. Sly foxes nipped at her ankles as she struggled through nightmarish swamps. Something cold and slimy slipped after her, just out of sight.

She woke early, unrested. Her breakfast went down like a cold lump. Her legs ached.

Ari stretched now, trying to loosen the tight muscles in her calves and thighs. She put her arms over her head and bent from the waist, touching her toes. "Chase and I should be able to handle the Council, Dr. Bohnes. And the extra two days is through a rough part of the forest. It will —" She bit her words off. The tough little vet was sensitive about her age. Ari didn't want to say what she was thinking. That the trip would prove too hard for her old nurse.

"The more of us there are, the safer we'll be," Dr. Bohnes said. "And with some of the animals of the forest on the Shifter's side, we're going to have to take extra measures for safety."

"You mean, sentries at night? That kind of thing?"

"That kind of thing. We don't have to worry here near Atalanta's Grove." She caught Ari's surprised glance. "Oh, yes, I know she came to you and spoke of the quest. I know what you and Chase have to do, and I'm going with you on that trip, too. We all need to stay together. We've been lucky so far but as soon as we leave the better-traveled highways, we're going to have to look sharp. My magic — such that it is — will let us know if any of the Shifter's army is around, but I can't count on it to tell us when an animal that's usually safe isn't."

Ari looked at Dr. Bohnes shyly. She knew the old lady had been her nurse in the days when her mother and father sat on the thrones of Balinor, but she still didn't recall her very well. She knew her better as the crusty vet who had taken care of the horses at Glacier River Farm. "What sort of magic do you do?" she asked. "I mean, if it's okay for you to tell me."

"Oh. A little bit of this. A little bit of that."

"Can you send someone through the Gap?"

"I? Certainly not! That takes a one-hundred-percent-committed wizard. I can cure warts. Make a few love potions. Help a cow give better milk." She gave Ari's cheek a cheerful rub. "Not anything like yours will be, when you retrieve the Royal Scepter. Certainly not like the Dreamspeaker's magic."

"And even she has limits," Ari echoed thoughtfully. "What about . . . the Old Mare of the Mountain?"

Dr. Bohnes straightened up with a jerk. Her fierce blue eyes held Ari's. "Oh, yes. There is that. There's a deep magic beyond the Celestial Valley. And the Old Mare is part of it. But none of us knows much about her. Now, Your Highness. Let's get packed up and rolling. It's a bit of a jaunt to Staines Falls, and the sun's almost over the hilltop."

"And we'll part company at Balinor Ford," Ari said firmly. "You and Lori and Toby will go to Balinor Village, and Chase and I to the Council."

"No, Your Highness."

"Yes, Dr. Bohnes." Ari took a deep breath, lowered her chin, and said in her most impressive imperial voice. "I command it."

Dr. Bohnes's bright blue eyes opened wide. She worked her jaw back and forth, as if chewing a bit of gum. Then she nodded and said without any expression at all: "So be it."

Ari let her breath out. "You don't mind?" she said anxiously. "I just feel it's for the best. Poor Lori is

41

so homesick, I feel sorry for her. We're going to have to find some way to get her back to Glacier River. If you can't do it, we'll have to find someone who can. In the meantime, I know she'll feel more at home in the village. She's afraid of the forest, afraid of the animals, afraid of everything here."

Dr. Bohnes wrapped Ari's blanket into a neat roll and tucked it into Chase's saddlebags.

"Dr. Bohnes?"

"Let me know when you wish to leave, Your Royal Highness." She bowed. It hurt Ari to see her sturdy form bent over in front of her. She took Dr. Bohnes gently by the shoulders, but the old lady lowered her head and walked away without a word. Ari felt Chase's presence behind. She turned and buried her face in his flank. "She's angry with me. But Chase, it's for the best."

"Perhaps," he said gravely. "There is a price that Royals pay, Ari. You have just seen part of it now. Your subjects must obey you. But they may not like you for it."

Ari watched Dr. Bohnes adjust the bridle on Toby's head. She buckled the throat latch, then the noseband, talking angrily all the while. Ari was too far away to hear, but she could guess they were talking about:

How bossy she was.
How ignorant of the realities of life.
How stubborn.

42

Ari ran her fingers through Chase's forelock. "I *knew* I wasn't going to like this Princess stuff," she said.

She liked it even less when the party split up, and they said their good-byes at Balinor Ford. Balinor Village lay less than a day's ride directly south across the river. To the south were clean clothes, baths, hot food, and Lincoln. Ari couldn't believe how much she missed her dog. To the north lay a swell of forbidding mountains, Staines Waterfall, and the giant red oak where the animals of the forest held Council. Farther north — she wasn't sure. Danger. Maybe even mortal danger.

She and Chase watched until Dr. Bohnes, Lori, and Toby had safely forded the river. Then they turned to their own task.

She walked Chase the first part of the way. The sun was pleasantly warm, and the sky was blue. They saw few animals: a pair of squirrels, a covey of guinea hens, an occasional glimpse of white-tailed deer in the scattered groves of trees. Toward afternoon, the sky began to darken with rain clouds. Ari flexed lightly to bring Chase to a halt. "How much farther, do you think?"

He raised his head, sensitive nostrils probing the air. "At this pace, we should reach it an hour or so after sunset."

"When does the Council meet?

"As soon as the sun goes down, on the last night of the crescent moon."

"I think I'd like to be there, to greet them as they arrive. Do you feel up to a canter?"

She felt him dance underneath her on the tips of his hooves. The muscles in his back rippled in anticipation. "I would welcome a canter, milady."

She cued him — tapped her left heel against his side, raised the right rein slightly, and he sprang into a steady, joyful canter that made the miles speed away. The road was straight and free of holes. When the rain started, the water ran off the road and into muddy ditches. Over the thundering sound of Chase's hooves, Ari called, "Who made this road?"

"I do not know, milady. It is called the Mountain Road, for that is where it leads. There are no villages or towns here, this far from Balinor itself. Perhaps the magic of the Forest Folk has created and maintained it."

In a little less than an hour, the rain increased to a downpour. Ari felt Chase check beneath her. "Do you want to stop?"

"No, but you do," he called back. "Your left leg is cramping, isn't it?"

It was, but Ari refused to give in to it. "It's fine. We'll go on. We're getting soaked enough as it is. I'd like to reach the cover of the trees as quickly as possible."

He said nothing more, but forged steadily on. Ari wondered if the day would come when Chase would refuse her. The laws governing a Bonded Pair were strict, that much she recalled of her life before the accident in the Gap. The human partner in a Bonded Pair was to be obeyed, as all riders should be obeyed by the steeds they ride, whether they are unicorns, horses, or even — as Ari had once seen at Glacier River — farm cows. A rider's cues were made with hands, feet, legs, and body balance. Communication about the animal's physical movements was limited.

As the road moved upward toward the mountains, Ari heard Chase's breathing change from its deep, easy rhythm to shorter, harder breaths. Only then did she allow herself the ease of a trot. She flexed him down and stretched her left leg in the stirrup.

Suddenly, Chase halted. His entire body quivered under her. He moved forward just as suddenly. Ari knew immediately that something was wrong.

"What is it, Chase?"

He said nothing, merely snorted. Then in her mind she heard, *There is something trailing us.*

"Following us?" Ari asked aloud.

Chase jerked impatiently.

What do you mean, trailing us? she thought at him.

Tracking us. Hunting us.

The hunt! Was it one of his own animals, turned traitor? Or was it some awful thing from the Shifter's army of demons and monsters?

Fear flooded her. Outwardly, she remained

45

calm, back straight, one hand casually laid on her knee — but near the scabbard that carried her father's knife. She held Chase's reins in the other hand, guiding him with her knees. Rain dripped down her back and plastered her hair across her cheeks. She cast a quick look at the surrounding forest. There. A large pine tree — perhaps a quarter of a mile ahead. If they could reach the tree before their stalker sprang — they might have a chance.

She felt it — a large, sinuous shadow gliding on the ground behind them.

She rode casually, afraid to make a sudden move. Afraid to force whatever it was into battle.

They reached the large pine tree. Out of the corner of her eye, she saw a metallic flash of scales. She dismounted quietly, her back to the trunk of the tree. She pulled her knife from its sheath and passed it in a slow half-circle. Beside her, Chase lowered his horn.

I hope it's not a snake, she thought at Chase. *Anything except a —*

It dropped from the tree, winding around Chase's neck with the terrible certainty of a hangman's noose. Chase reared, trumpeting his battle cry. Ari shrieked with rage. She sprang up, knife poised to slash, but her great stallion was too tall. The serpent — at least two feet thick and fifteen feet long, wound its scaly length tighter and tighter around the unicorn's neck. Chase's eyes bulged. His war cry was cut off. Ari leaped and leaped again. Her left leg gave way. She fell hard against the tree, her breath knocked from her lungs.

The snake's head was diamond-shaped, its eyes flat, black, and evil. A long red tongue flicked from its mouth, a sinister whip with poison at the tip.

Ari scrambled up the tree, skinning her hands raw on the bark. She reached the lowest branch and swung her leg over it. Below her, Chase plunged and reared, his struggle silent now.

Closer, Chase! Come closer!

He rolled his eyes, dark with agony, then whirled and smashed his body against the tree trunk. Ari bent far out from the branch, her father's knife in her right hand, her left clutching the punishing bark. She slashed at the flat black eyes, knowing that this was the most vulnerable part of the snake, that she had no hope of slashing that ropy scaliness free from Chase.

"Ariiii-aaaa-nnnnaaaa!" it hissed.

"You get OFF him!" she panted. "You leave him alone!" She reached out with the knife again, too far this time, and fell.

Instinctively, she rolled herself into a ball, protecting her already scarred legs from further hurt. She landed with a thump at the base of the tree, slamming her head against a gnarled root. Above her, Chase whirled and spun, ducked and

47

kicked. With a sudden, ferocious burst of power, he swung his neck against the tree. The snake's head connected with the trunk with an audible thud.

"It's stunned! Chase! It's stunned!" She pushed herself to her feet and fell into Chase's flank. His side was slippery with sweat. Gasping, she pulled at the suddenly inert length of scales, tugging the snake's body free from Chase's neck. The reptile landed in the grass, mouth open, thin red tongue lolling from its jaws.

"Is it dead?" Ari asked in a half-whisper.

Chase's head was low. He breathed in great gulps of air. Grasping her knife firmly, Ari crept closer. She held her breath.

The flat black eyes snapped open. The snake struggled weakly, then fell back. It looked at her. The look was as cold and as venomous as Ari had ever seen. "Come closssser," it whispered. "Closssser."

Ari held her knife up, so that the snake could see it. "I'll use this," she threatened. She edged nearer carefully. Above her, Chase gasped and coughed. "Who are you?" she demanded. "Who sent you? Where do you come from?"

"Princessss," it hissed. "Oh, Princessss. My massssster would have sssspeech with you. Ssssome-time. Ssssometime. Perhapssss. In the Valley. Come to the Valley."

The black eyes looked inward for a long,

long moment. Then, with a flick of its red tongue, a last, ugly hiss, it slid from view into the forest. Ari covered her face with her hands. She was shaking so hard her teeth were chattering. Chase buried his muzzle in her hair.

"We fought it off," he said.

"What about the next time?" Ari said. "And the time after that? Oh, Chase. I don't think I can do this. I'm so afraid!"

He didn't speak for a moment. The rain dripped from the trees. It grew colder. Ari leaned against the warmth of Chase's body. Finally, her shivering stopped.

"Are you ready?" Chase asked. His voice was deep and kind.

"No, I'm not ready," Ari said bitterly. "I'll never be ready. I didn't ask for this, Chase. I didn't want to be the Princess!"

"But you are," Chase said. "And the Council waits for us. If you decide, Arianna, that we cannot do this, then I will go with you wherever you wish. Back to Glacier River Farm, to teach young humans to ride. Or back to Balinor or some small village where we can live in peace. Where no one will know who we are."

Ari wiped her face. She took a long shuddering breath. "No," she said. "I'm not letting a miserable snake stand in the way of peace in Balinor."

He blew out a soft sound, the way a unicorn

mare comforts a foal. "Perhaps there will be peace," he said. "If we don't give up."

Ari nodded. She remounted. They climbed the last rocky path to Staines Falls and the giant red oak tree.

They had reached the Council.

6

It was very peaceful and lonesome. A brisk wind blew in the treetops. But the trees were so old and so tall, the air around the Council place was still. The waterfall was slow and quiet. It slipped into a rock pool with the gentlest of sounds. The red oak was gnarly, twisted, full of strange and wonderful whorls in the bark. Beneath it was a large piece of granite rock, polished to a flat smoothness on top, ringed round with fossil stones at the base. The area around the red oak tree and the granite rock was covered in grass as smooth and short as if someone had scythed it.

She followed Chase's lead. He walked majestically to the foot of the oak. He bent his head and dipped his horn in the water: once, twice, three times. The water sparkled and shone.

A memory came to Ari, a story about the magic of a unicorn's horn. The touch of the horn made foul water sweet, turned muddy streams to clear pools. All of a sudden, Ari was thirsty. As thirsty as she'd ever been before. She knelt at the pool, cupped her hands, and drank. The taste was sweet, cold, like drinking rain clouds. Her tiredness and fear ebbed away. She felt strong, clearheaded. More, she told herself, like a Princess than she had felt before.

Chase settled himself at the base of the tree, hind legs tucked under his belly, his forelegs knuckled under his chest. Ari sat down a little way from him, her back against the granite rock.

They waited.

The animals came slowly to the Council. First was a pair of foxes: the male fox, a vibrant red with a black mask and golden eyes, and the vixen, a multicolored swirl of brown, cream, and gray. They sat quietly at the edge of the meadow. Then came the deer, timid and graceful. A raccoon, with a clever, merry face. *Three bears — just like the fairy tale!* Ari thought. A huge black male, a smaller dun-colored female, and a cub, who chattered and giggled until his mother pushed him gently down onto his father's back. He clung there, button eyes bright, and hummed a tiny song to himself.

The meadow was full by the time the sun went down. The pool was filled with otter and beaver. The crescent moon was thin, pale, and shed no light. The Sunchaser was a vivid spot of bronze in the gloom. The ruby jewel glowed crimson at the base of his horn. The animals faded into shadow, and all Ari could see was the occasional flash of a yellow eye. She thought she saw Sandy and Rufus and Tige in the gathering pack of wolves, but she wasn't certain.

There was a murmur and a shifting. The pad of heavy feet.

A lion came into the clearing.

He was big, heavy with muscle, and slow with the confidence of the strong and powerful. He came very near Ari on his way to the base of the tree. She caught a heavy, musky scent as the lion passed by.

He stopped in front of Chase. The unicorn looked full into the lion's wild eyes. Then he rose to his full height, towering over the lion, his ebony horn a vivid black against the dusky twilight.

"My lord," the lion said. He braced himself with his heavy forepaws. Slowly, deliberately, he settled onto his side, then rolled over on his back, exposing his belly to the Sunchaser's sharp horn. Ari blinked. Even the lion showed obedience to the Sunchaser! She tried not to laugh at the thought of Balinor villagers rolling over like that to show their loyalty; it was a good thing people and animals were different.

"Vanax. My friend and adviser," Chase answered. "It is good to see you again."

Vanax rolled to his feet. "And it is good to see you again, Sunchaser, Lord of the Animals. Bonded to the Royal House of Balinor. The animals of the forest welcome you." A chorus of growls, yips, bleats, and snuffles from the others followed.

Chase waited gravely until the salutations died away. "I have been gone too long. I have returned to disappointment and despair. There are fewer of our brothers and sisters here than there have ever been before. I do not see the cougars. The ferrets are absent. And others. Too many. They have joined the hunt?"

The tip of Vanax's tail twitched back and forth. He growled, low in his throat. "Yes, Your Majesty."

Chase's eye darkened in anger. "There are laws against the hunt. Since humans and animals first celebrated the Bond. It is so."

"It is so," the forest creatures responded.

"The punishment is the breaking of the Bond. Those animals who hunt will be forever mute. Before judgment is passed, are there those who would speak for the traitors?"

An uneasy silence fell over the Council. Finally, a voice from the back hissed out: "They are afraid to sssspeak!"

Ari jumped. She knew that voice! The snake!

"All may speak without fear at Council," the Sunchaser said gravely. "This is neutral ground. Any may come and go at will."

"Proof!" the snake called out. "Proof of aaaamnessssty." Ari narrowed her eyes and searched the dimness of the meadow. Was it there, the creature? In that hedge of sumac?

"My word is proof enough," Chase said angrily.

An undulating hiss came from the sumac. The snake laughed. "Fool!" it murmured. Then, with barely a ripple of the leaves, it glided into the center of the grounds. Yellow-green scales glittered poisonously in the low light. The snake regarded Chase with lidless eyes. "Ssssunchaser!" it mocked. "Lord of the Animalsssss. Phhhha!" The red tongue flicked the air. The snake rose on its tail like a cobra and began to sway back and forth. "My masssster callssss you all to the hunt! You, Vanax!" The lion's tail twitched faster and faster. "Do you not dream of the hunt at night? And you, Basil. Dill." The pair of foxes jumped and snarled at the snake. "Do not your eyessss and nossssessss enticccce you to follow the tracks of a nice juicy *rabbit*?" The snake stood still. Its lipless mouth stretched into a grin. "Thissss is the right way. The way of prey. My masssster will give thissss to all who wish to join him."

"It is not the way of Balinor," Chase said gravely. "Is this all you have in the way of defense, Snake? That the evil ways of the Shifter are just?"

"It issss all the defensssse we need," the snake said. "It is jusssst becaussssse the hunt issss in our nature. Come! Bear! Fox! Cougar! Join ussss and be free!"

"Join the Shifter and become mute forever,"

Chase said. "The bonds with humans will be broken past retrieving. That is the punishment."

"Oh?" The snake swiveled suddenly. Its eyes glowed red. "And how will you accomplisssssh *that*, great one? Mighty unicorn. *Powerful* one!" It laughed again. Ari's skin crawled. "You have no magic! Thissss one," it hissed, ducking its head toward Ari. "Thissss one is only the sssshell of a Princessss. Sssshe hassss no power!"

"Not yet," Ari said. She stood up. Her knees were shaking, but her voice was clear and firm. "But I shall retrieve the Scepter, snake. And when I do, all will be right in Balinor."

"Sssso you sssseek my masssster? You — and that four-legged fool! We await you, Princessss. We look forward to it. We will welcome you, Arianna, to the Valley of Fear!" To Ari's terrified eyes, the snake grew larger and larger. Its scaly body seemed to fill the grove. Then with a last, thin laugh, it slid away into the brush.

Vanax growled. His haunches clenched and his powerful claws dug into the grass.

"No," Chase said. "Do not pursue the snake. All are guaranteed safety here, Vanax. This is not a place for battle." Vanax half-closed his eyes and opened them again. He sank unhappily to the ground.

"Sire?" The red fox — Basil, the snake had called him — came forward. "Is it true? You and Her

Highness Arianna are not in possession of your full powers?"

"Not yet," Chase said. "And the snake is right. We need the Royal Scepter."

Ari took a deep breath. "And we will find it," she said.

"You are going to the Valley of Fear?" Basil asked.

"We must." Ari hoped she didn't sound as scared as she felt.

"Oh, my." The fox rubbed his pointed nose with his paw. "Oh, *my*!" The vixen darted up beside him, and gave him a sharp nudge. "For goodness' sake, Basil, get a grip."

"Don't *shove* me, Dill," the fox said crossly.

"I'll shove you when I please," Dill shot back. "I'll shove you whenever I like. I say, if Her Royal Highness and His Majesty are going on a quest to the Valley of Fear, then, of course they'll get the Scepter back. Just because the place is filled with shadow unicorns and ghouls . . ."

"Monsters," Basil said gloomily.

"Hideous mutants!" Dill added. "That doesn't mean that one unicorn and one Princess won't be able to find the lair of the Shifter, battle the shadow herd, find their way out again, and bring the Scepter to safety."

"When you put it like that, Dill —"

"I'll put it any way I like, Basil."

"— it doesn't seem safe for them to go alone."

Dill nodded in satisfaction. "Right!" She turned to Ari, ducked her head in a short bow, and said, "You need an army, Your Royal Highness."

Ari blinked. At the moment, her mind filled with the visions of shadow unicorns, ghouls, mutants, and monsters, an army seemed like a very good idea.

"There *is* the question of how," Basil said fussily. "I mean, an army is all very well and good, Dill. But who's going to join up? Where are the weapons going to come from?"

Dill yawned casually, showing her pointed teeth.

"Us?" Basil yelped. "You want us to be the army?"

"Just think for a minute, Basil." She turned and addressed Ari with a casual flip of her tail. "We might even see if we can coax Noki the dragon out of her cave for once. . . ."

"She's gained a lot of weight," Basil said doubtfully.

"But she's a dragon," Dill said, "and everyone's afraid of dragons, even those in the Valley of Fear. Honestly, Basil, can't you agree with me just *once* without some stupid argument?"

"Stop," a voice behind Chase said. "There will be no army."

"No army!" Dill narrowed her eyes at Chase. It

was clear she thought the voice came from him. Her thick gray fur bristled. "Huh! You *need* an army. You can't *do* this without an army. You'll get mashed, crushed, smooshed, and obliterated without an army!" Abruptly, she noticed the scowl in Chase's eyes. "Sorry, Your Majesty," she added hastily. She sank to the ground in confusion.

"Now you've done it, Dill," Basil muttered.

"Listen to me!"

Ari and Chase turned around, looking for who had spoken, but no one was there. Ari leaned back against the granite rock. Then she leaped forward. The rock was alive!

Ari backed into Chase. The granite rock swelled with the heavy breathing of an animal. Slowly . . . slowly, the rock softened and took shape in the summer dark.

It was a unicorn. An old gray unicorn. The hair in her ears was stiff and white. Her back was swayed. Her horn was short and chipped in places. Whiskers covered her chin. But her eyes! Her eyes were youthful, clear, and as transparent as water.

Beside her, Chase sank to his knees and touched his horn to the ground. Ari looked around the clearing. Vanax covered his eyes with his paws. Dill's head was buried in Basil's flank. Basil himself stared at the old unicorn in awe.

"The Old Mare of the Mountain!" someone whispered.

"Well!" the Old Mare said. She coughed, a deep, hollow cough. She stretched her neck forward. "Armies! Never heard such nonsense in all my life!"

Ari wasn't sure where it came from — or even why she felt it, but the Old Mare of the Mountain radiated power and strength. Ari felt very small in the presence of this being. The ancient body, the scraggly coat, the stiff, whiskery hair, all cloaked a magnificent power.

Ari held her breath, then asked softly, "Milady? The Dreamspeaker said you might come. If it is you."

The unicorn stopped scratching her ear, put her hind leg down, and peered at Ari.

"But . . . are you the Old Mare of —" Ari started to ask.

"Be still." The voice was thunder. It filled the Council grove. The animals moaned.

Ari swallowed hard. The old unicorn swung her head slowly back and forth. She settled onto the ground and curled up like a unicorn foal. She began to turn back into rock. The granite crept up her sides, across her flanks, moved up her neck. But her eyes remained locked on Ari's: clear, young, vibrant eyes.

She said, "Now that I think about it. Yes. I am the Old Mare." She yawned, showing yellow teeth, worn by years of grazing. "And I have a word for you. Or two."

Ari, hypnotized, gazed into those clear, clear eyes.

"Pay attention, human child!"

Ari jumped. The Old Mare's voice was suddenly booming, shaking the trees.

"Six shall find the Scepter Royal,
The quick, the smart, the brave, the loyal.
Of humans there shall be but two,
One young and one whose past is new.
Of Six who go, two wait to learn,
Three of Six shall not return."

The gigantic booming voice stopped. And then the Old Mare was gone, or her physical body was. Turned back into rock. Ari walked up to the boulder and touched it. Stone. Cold stone.

Chase rose to his feet.

"Oh!" Ari said. "Did you see that? She just . . . just . . . showed up and then, poof!" Ari snapped her fingers. "What do you suppose . . . why, Chase! You're trembling." Concerned, she put her hands on his neck. He was sweating.

"The deep magic," Dill said in a hushed voice. She trotted briskly up to them, her face alive with excitement. "The deep magic! I saw it!"

"Do not speak of it, Dill," Basil whispered. He'd been deeply affected by the Old Mare. Ari looked around the clearing. All the animals were shocked, stunned. Some of them sat and stared, others talked quietly among themselves.

"It was a message for you, Your Royal Highness," Dill said respectfully. "Ah, to think I lived to see this. Most of us would not expect to see the deep magic once in a lifetime. Not once in *three* lifetimes."

"I see," Ari said, although she didn't, not really. What was she supposed to do with this message? She would think about it later, she decided. Right now, she needed the assistance of the forest animals. "Now, what about this army, Chase? I think it's a pretty good idea, myself."

"'Six shall find the Scepter Royal,'" Dill quoted. "No armies for us, Your Royal Highness. She said six. And she meant six."

"The Valley of Fear sounds like a terrible place," Ari said frankly. "But we *have* to get that Scepter. Our odds will be better if we have an army behind us."

Dill stared at her. Rather rudely, Ari thought. "It's the deep magic," she repeated loudly, as if to a child. "'Six shall find . . .'"

"Yes, yes," Ari said, "I heard."

"Her Highness does not have all of her memory," Chase said. He'd recovered from the shock of the Old Mare's visitation. "We are hoping — that is, the Dreamspeaker has said that the Princess will recall everything of her former life when the Scepter is in her hands." He bent his head. His dark eyes looked directly into Ari's. "We have no choice, milady. The Old Mare has told us the way. She has told us what must be."

"Oh." Ari rubbed her forehead. "Then we go into the Valley of Fear with just six? Which six?"

"'The quick, the smart, the brave —'" Dill said. "That's pretty obvious to me. The quick is Basil, here. I'm the smart one."

"Excuse me, Dill," Basil said. "But it's the other way around. I'm the smart one."

"No, you aren't."

"Yes, I am!"

"No, you're not!"

"Excuse me," Ari said. "But I think it's safe to say that we're all pretty smart here."

"Not as smart as I am," Dill said smugly. "*I've* been to the Valley of Fear!"

There was a short, impressed silence from everyone.

"I'm smart because I can show you the way after we get there. And because I got out alive, which is more than I can say for some." Her gold eyes darkened. She was in the grip of some unpleasant memory. She shook herself briskly, and Ari noticed for the first time a thin red scar around Dill's neck.

"We need to take apart the message and figure out what it means," Dill said. "His Majesty, the

Sunchaser, is the *brave* one. And you, Your Royal Highness, are the one whose *past is new* — because you don't have all your memory yet. Now, as far as *loyal* goes, well, that could be any one of us here — we're all loyal to the Crown. And the young one." She frowned. "I don't like the idea of having a youngster with us. I don't even know which youngster it would be. I'm sure that the Old Mare would not send a cub into danger without a good reason."

"It will not be a cub," Chase said. "It will be a human. She prophesied two humans. And as for loyalty — there is one other who is loyal to the Princess unto death, besides myself. But he is not with us."

"Do you mean Lincoln?" Ari asked. She so wanted to see her collie again! "Of course. And the young human — oh, Chase! Lori absolutely will not go. She'll think we're out of our minds!"

7

"**Y**ou're out of your mind!" Lori yelled. "Go with you to this Valley of Fear place? Are you *crazy*?" She stamped up and down the length of her room at the Inn of the Unicorn. Lincoln the collie, with only a shaved patch on his forehead to show he'd been deeply wounded after fighting off an attack on Arianna, yawned deeply and snuggled against Ari's side. Ari stroked his ears, and tried to explain for the third time why they needed Lori with them.

The trip to Balinor Village had taken Chase and Ari less than a day at a canter. They had left the forest early in the morning following the Council of the Animals, bidding farewell to those who had remained to discuss the events of the meeting. At the outskirts of the village, they took care to be as inconspicuous as possible. They had gone straight to the Inn of the Unicorn, where Dr. Bohnes, Lincoln, and Mr. Samlett, the Innkeeper, had greeted them with joy. Lori wasn't particularly happy to see them again — and was really *un*happy when Ari told her of the Old Mare's Prophecy: that they had to pack up and leave for the Valley of Fear. Right now.

"No!" she shouted for what seemed to be the thousandth time. "No! No! NO!"

Dr. Bohnes, her lips compressed in a tight line, kept on packing the bedrolls. She heard Chase and Ari's news. Then she heaved a sigh straight from the bottom of her leather boots. "If it was the Old Mare — and, oh, I wish I'd seen her myself! — you don't have a choice. You're right. You have to leave, and leave right away. Samlett will drive. Toby will take you in the cart to the shore of the Sixth Sea, and from there you can get a ship to take you to Demon-view, gateway to the Valley of Fear. I'll help you pack."

"Lori. Please try to understand." Ari leaned forward in yet another attempt to make the blond girl understand. "If we go with five, it doesn't fulfill the Prophecy. Six of us must go. I told you there's a total of five who have agreed to go. You're the sixth."

"Tough!" Lori kicked at the wooden bench in front of the fireplace. "Who cares? You want to go roaming around in a place like this Valley of Fear, you go right ahead. But count me out!" She gave the bench a final kick, whirled around, and slammed out the door.

Ari wrapped her arms around her knees and stared into the fire.

What were they going to do now?

8

Atalanta lifted her head from the scene in the Watching Pool, a thoughtful expression clouding her violet eyes. At her forefeet, the clear waters of the pool swirled briefly and the image of the Princess, the collie, and Eliane Bohnes faded into the depths. Beside her, Tobiano sniffed disapprovingly. "I knew Lori wouldn't go," he said with glum satisfaction. "Now we are in trouble."

"Perhaps." Then Atalanta quoted softly, "'Three of Six shall not return.' What do you think the Old Mare meant by that?"

Toby shook his head.

"We have questions," Atalanta said to herself. "Questions with answers as hidden as the sun during storms. There is the Shifter himself, Tobiano. He knows that the Six will come, but he doesn't know when. And he can only guess at who the Six will be. Then there is that dog, Lincoln. Who gave the collie the ruby jewel to take to Arianna back at Glacier River Farm, Toby? I have not yet found an answer to that. The dog bothers me."

"If you don't know," Toby said with perfect truth, "who would?"

"The Old Mare. Some of this is part of the deep magic. Perhaps the dog is part of the deep magic. Perhaps not."

"Pretty amazing," Toby said. "That the Old Mare showed up like that. If she hadn't intervened, we would have had a whole army of animals storming the Valley of Fear. And no one's anywhere near ready to fight."

"Not so amazing," Atalanta said with a slight smile. "Toby? You behaved with great courage down below in Balinor. You were quite heroic."

The stout little unicorn puffed out his chest. The Celestial unicorns were at risk in the world of humans — vulnerable to hurt, to illness, and worst of all, to death. Celestials who spent too much time below in Balinor could lose the unicorn's most precious gift: immortality. But Toby had bravely agreed when Atalanta had asked him to accompany the Princess and the Sunchaser, despite the risk to himself.

"May I send you back to Balinor? Just one more time?"

Toby didn't hesitate, a testament to his courage. "To go into the Valley of Fear? To be one of the Six! Yes, Dreamspeaker!"

"No. Not to the Valley of Fear. Arianna is right. Lori must go with them to the Valley of Fear, and no one else. I want you to go below to help Princess Arianna get to the Sixth Sea. And you must be alert to danger."

"What kind of danger?" he asked suspiciously.

Atalanta gazed at him. The black-and-white unicorn was the rudest herdmate they had ever had. But Atalanta was convinced he had the bravest, most loyal heart of them all. "Danger of the worst kind."

9

Lori stamped into the stable yard at the back of the Inn of the Unicorn. She was furious, confused, and homesick.

She sat on the edge of the watering trough and tossed bits of straw into the water. Mr. Samlett bustled by, trundling a wheelbarrow filled with manure from the stalls. "Now, milady, quit that, I say quit that," he exclaimed. "The trough will just have to be cleaned up again. Her Highness will not like that at all, I say not at all."

"Fine!" Lori said crossly. She got up. "That's just fine!" She crossed the cobblestones with the air of knowing where she was headed, just in case Samlett asked her to clean the trough herself.

"Milady?" he called after her. Lori turned around. His round, red face had an apologetic frown on it. "I'm sorry to bring this up, milady, but about your bill for room and board . . ."

"Ask Her Royal Highness!" Lori shouted furiously.

Samlett dropped the handles of the wheelbarrow with a thump. Straw scattered all over the footpath. "Ssssh!" he whispered. "No one is to know she's here!"

"That *who's* here?" asked a smooth, caressing voice. Lady Kylie rounded the corner of the Inn. She was dressed in chocolate-colored velvet, beaded with pearls. Her black hair was caught up in an elaborate gold-mesh net. She looked rich. She looked as if no one had ever bugged *her* about a bill for a crummy, sagging bed and a few bowls of lousy vegetable stew.

"Hey," Lori said, by way of greeting. She had become friends with the smooth-voiced woman while Ari and her pals had been off on one of their busybody trips trying to regain power over this so-called kingdom. She'd been to Lady Kylie's mansion — well, it was her brother's manor — for lunch a few times. She kept hoping that Lady Kylie would ask her to stay. Lord Lexan's manor was a lot nicer than this crummy Inn.

Lady Kylie had been very interested in Ari's adventures on the other side of the Gap. Lori had told her that Ari was just a stable hand at Glacier River Farm. And that *there*, she, Lori, was the important one. Her father, Lori said, was as rich as Lady Kylie's brother. Maybe even richer. And he wouldn't

71

have stood for the way Lori was being treated around *here* for one little second.

"We aren't supposed to know that *who* is here?" Lady Kylie asked in her creamy-voiced way.

"Well, don't tell anybody," Lori said, "but —"

"Lori!" Toby trotted into the stable yard. His withers were damp with sweat. It looked as if he had run long and hard to get there. Lori made a face at him. He'd left her and Dr. Bohnes at the edge of the village two days ago, and she'd thought she'd seen the last of him.

"Ah! Tobiano!" Kylie purred. "How good to see you again."

"The last time I saw you, you were having a bit of trouble getting your unicorns to take you home," Toby said. "Things a bit different now?"

"Yes," she said shortly.

"They're talking again, those two. Must be a lot easier to go from place to place, now that your animals can talk to you again," Toby said with a grin.

"He may have his *horn*," Kylie hissed furiously, "but my masssster has the power!" Her flat black eyes glittered with malevolence.

"Are you talking about Chase?" Lori said, mainly to avoid being ignored.

"Your master is going to lose. And lose big," Toby said shortly. "I'd get back home if I were you."

Lady Kylie raised one thin black eyebrow. "You would?" she asked softly. "And then what? Prepare for a journey, perhaps?"

"Stay home, is my advice," Toby said. "If you know what's good for you."

Lady Kylie fingered the elaborate knife at her belt. "Ah, now, Tobiano. Why would I want to remain at home? When I and my fellows can hunt?"

"What *are* you two talking about?!" Lori demanded.

"Unicorn stew?" Kylie said. "Perhaps. Perhaps not. Good day to you, Tobiano." She turned to Lori. She placed a hand on the blond girl's sleeve. Her nails were long and painted bloodred. "Stop by," she hissed. "Before you leave. Yes?"

"Um, I guess so," Lori said uncomfortably. "But I'm not going anywhere." She glared at Toby. "Not anywhere."

"Beat it, Kylie," Toby said. "If you know what's good for you."

Lady Kylie looked around, as if to gauge her chances. Mr. Samlett stared at her from the door of the stables. Two draft unicorns, their heavy necks thick with muscle, gazed at her from the open doors of their stalls. She nodded to herself, gave them all a nasty smile, then glided away.

"That's a gorgeous dress she's wearing," Lori said.

Toby snorted. "Now, miss," he said sternly. "I have a message for you. You are going on that trip. And you're not going to tell anyone but Ari and Chase why."

10

"I'm glad you've decided to go with us," Ari said gravely. They were in the great room downstairs at the Inn. Lori had been out all afternoon. When she came back, she seemed in good spirits. And she told Ari that she would be one of the Six.

The light was failing and night was coming on. It was the first night of the Shifter's Moon — which meant, of course, no moon.

"I don't want to go, thank you very much. But Toby says I can go back through the Gap — he's not sure how. He thinks some old unicorn is going to take care of it. All he would say is 'it's part of the deep magic' — and stuff like that. Anyway, I'm going. And I'm telling you, I'm not doing anything but riding along. No getting wood for the fire, no cooking. Nothing. Got it?"

Ari nodded. "Toby said that three of the Six will be sent through the Gap?"

"That's what this Prophecy means, supposedly." Lori picked up a peach from the wooden bowl on the sideboard. She bit into it. Peach juice ran down her chin.

Ari said, " 'Of Six who go, two wait to learn, Three of Six shall not return.' "

"Toby said the other one who gets to go home is Lincoln." Lori tossed the peach pit back into the wooden bowl. "He's not supposed to be here, either."

I do not wish to go back! Lincoln gazed up at Ari with worried eyes. *I want to stay with you.* His bronze-and-black coat was ruffled.

Ari bent over and smoothed Lincoln's fur with her hands. She swallowed hard. She bit her lip, then whispered into one tulip ear, "Being Princess is so *hard*, Linc." She grabbed his white ruff with both hands and shook it gently. Then without looking at Lori, she said evenly, "Did Toby think that there was another meaning to the Prophecy?"

"Like what?"

Ari got up and faced her. "It's dangerous. What we're about to do. The future of the Kingdom hangs in the balance." Then, seeing that Lori still didn't get it, she said, "Lives are at stake. We may be killed."

"Yeah. He said that. But I'm telling you, I'll travel with you, but I'm not doing more than that. I won't fight. I won't lift a finger against that guy, the Shifter."

"That may not matter to him."

Lori looked smug, but didn't say anything more.

Ari shrugged. "Okay. I've warned you. Are you ready to go?"

Lori widened her eyes. "Now? We can't go now. I told . . . I mean, I thought we should wait until after this Shifter's Moon thing is over."

"We'll go now."

"I can't go right this minute," Lori said sulkily. "I have to say good-bye to . . . to . . . my friends. And I have to pack my stuff."

"There's no need to wait any longer," Ari said patiently. "The foxes Dill and Basil have been waiting by Balinor Ford since this afternoon. We'll stop and pick them up. I won't sleep tonight, anyway, and we'll be less conspicuous in the dark."

"I'm *not* going now." Lori folded her arms across her chest. "I'm spending the night in a real bed. I'll think about leaving in the morning."

Ari marched over to her. She grabbed Lori's shoulders in both hands and stared directly into her face. Ari dropped her voice to a fierce whisper. "You. Will. Do. What. I. Say." She punctuated each word with a little shake of Lori's shoulders. Lori's mouth dropped open. "I've agreed to your terms, Lori. Now listen to mine. If you want to survive this journey, you will do exactly what I say exactly when I say it. You got that?"

Lori nodded, too shocked to speak.

"Good," Ari chirruped softly. "Linc? Let's go." She turned on her heel. "You've got five minutes, Lori. Then the cart leaves without you."

Ari went back to her room to collect her saddlebags and say good-bye to Dr. Bohnes. The little old vet kissed her firmly on both cheeks, then pressed a small bag into her hand. "My magic is for small things," she said. She chuckled, her face breaking into a thousand wrinkles. "A little bit of this. A little bit of that."

"Magic," Ari said. "Thank you." She had two talismans now. The Star Bottle with Atalanta's water, and this little bag. She started to open it. Bohnesy's strong hand closed over her arm. "Use it when there's no way out! Get going now, Princess." If there were tears, she didn't let Ari see them. "And *you*," she scolded the collie. "Keep watch over her!"

Lincoln barked. Ari picked up her saddlebags, then left her room to tap on Lori's door. When the blond girl came out, she was dressed in a brown velvet dress.

"Wow," Ari said. "That's an amazing outfit. Did Samlett give that to you?"

Lori avoided a direct answer. "He said we had to travel in disguise, at least until we reach the Sixth Sea. So I said the best disguise would be if you were my maid. Remember how we first came to

Balinor? You were my maid then." She smoothed the dark velvet with a complacent air. "So you can be my maid now."

Ari didn't bother to correct her. When they had first arrived in Balinor Village, Mr. Samlett had assumed Ari was Lori's maid because Lori had refused to walk and was riding Chase. Ari led the way downstairs, carrying Lori's sack of clothes — as well as her own saddlebags — to avoid further argument. Mr. Samlett was waiting outside in the cart. Toby was in the harness. He nodded to them as the two girls and the dog came out the back door.

Chase stood a short distance away. He was haltered, but had no saddle or bridle. They were traveling light, and the tack would be an encumbrance. If Ari had to ride, she'd ride bareback.

Ari had been worried that Chase would be recognized on their journey to Sixton, the village that lay on the shore of the Sixth Sea. So she had rubbed kitchen grease all over his beautiful bronze coat, dulling his brilliant glow to a muddy brown. She'd covered the glowing ruby jewel at the base of his horn with a couple of dabs of black paint. But there wasn't much she could do about his size — larger than any other unicorn in Balinor — or his magnificent walk.

Mr. Samlett glanced anxiously at the sky. The moon was dark — the first night of the four days of the Shifter's Moon. "You sure you want to start out *now*, Your Royal Highness? No *good* magic works in these hours."

"It's best," Ari said. "Our enemies won't expect us to leave at this time. We'll increase our chances of traveling unnoticed."

"It'll take two days to reach the Sixth Sea, milady," Mr. Samlett said. "Depends on the state of the roads. We're to leave you there, according to Toby. You know where you're goin' from there? I say, you know where you're goin'?"

"Best not to ask, Samlett," Chase said.

"That's right, Your Majesty. I won't. Only Sixton is somewhat a rough town from all accounts."

Chase lifted his ebony horn. The sharp end glinted in the starlight. "We are well-protected," he said.

Lincoln stationed himself at Chase's left. Lori and Ari climbed into the cart. Mr. Samlett had covered the bottom with thick quilts, and it was actually quite comfortable. There was a roof over the cart, held up by four sturdy posts at the corners. Two lanterns hung at the rear. They were so bright, Ari could have read a book — if she had anything to read — which she didn't. She sighed. She hadn't read anything for weeks. And she missed it. A long, narrow chest was tucked under the driver's perch. Ari leaned over and opened it: provisions! Thick sandwiches, peaches, flasks of lemonade, several pies. They had enough for a week's journey!

"Are you ready, Your Royal Highness?"

"Ready."

Mr. Samlett slapped the reins against Toby's rump and said "Gee-yup!" Toby moved out at a rapid walk. The cart rumbled on the cobblestones.

They were off.

Ari sat with her knees up, back braced against a cushion propped against the side of the cart. She was wearing her breeches underneath the red skirt. She fingered the skirt material and sighed to herself. It was so nice to have some clean clothes and something different to wear. Like Lori's brown velvet dress. If she ever regained the throne — no, she told herself firmly, she *was* going to regain the throne, it was best to take a positive attitude — the one Royal privilege she was going to allow herself was new clothes. She wriggled her toes inside her riding boots. They were worn and cracked after all her adventures. And new shoes. She hoped there was a Royal Shoemaker. If not, one of her first Royal acts was going to be hiring one.

"Why are we stopping?" Lori asked nervously.

Ari jerked herself out of her musings. Samlett had pulled the cart over. They must be at Balinor Ford already. "We're picking up two more passengers," she said. "Basil and Dill."

Lori sniffed disapprovingly. "This cart is already too small —" She interrupted herself, and said with interest, "Did you say Basil? We're picking up a guy? Is he cute?"

"Well, he's male," Ari said, choking back a laugh. "And he's got gorgeous red hair. But he's — um — committed already, you might say." She stood up and peered into the darkness. Balinor River rippled softly under the starlight. The area around the ford was broad and flat. Ari didn't see any sign of the fox and vixen. Then she heard a splash from the riverbank, and a pair of familiar voices.

"I told you, didn't I? Let *me* catch the fish, I said. Honestly, Basil. You are so *lame*! I told you what would happen if you leaned over too far."

"You *pushed* me, Dill."

"I did not."

"You did too."

"I did —"

"Dill?" Ari called softly. "Basil? We're here!"

"NOT!" Dill concluded triumphantly. "We'll be right there, Your Royal Highness."

Ari heard the sound of energetic swimming, the sound of little bodies splooshing out of the mud, a short, furious squabble, and both foxes leaped into the wagon.

Lori jumped up and screamed. Ari grabbed her forearm and said sternly, "*Be quiet!*" She released Lori's arm. "Dill? Basil? This is Lori Carmichael."

Dill sat on her haunches and looked Lori up

and down. "Hmm," she said. "You know who she reminds me of, Basil? That little brat of a ferret that lived one meadow over when we had our den in Luckon. Same shifty look to her."

"Hey!" Lori said indignantly.

Basil, whose dark red fur was wet and muddy, put his paws on Lori's riding habit so that he could stretch up and see her face more clearly. Lori opened her mouth to scream, cast a hasty look at Ari, then settled for pushing Basil away with her toe. "Ugh!" she muttered.

"She doesn't look at all like that ferret. That ferret had dark brown fur and beady brown eyes."

"She's got beady *blue* eyes," Dill said. "Don't argue with me, Basil."

"I'm not arguing with you, Dill."

"You are *too!*"

"Stop, please," Ari said pleasantly. "It's a long journey to Sixton and the shore of the Sixth Sea, Dill. We have plans to make on the way. First, I want to know everything there is to know about the Valley of Fear. The best defense is to be prepared. I'd like to create a map, so that we can all see where we're headed."

Dill, for once, was completely quiet. She looked up at the night sky. The moon was dark — the Shifter's Moon. The stars seemed faded and far away. "I'll tell you what I know, Your Royal Highness," she said. "But not now. Not now. Tomorrow, when the sun is bright, and we won't imagine things coming after us in the dark."

"Tomorrow, then," Ari said. "Tonight, wc may as well sleep while we can." She raised her voice, "Mr. Samlett? Shall we find a place to pull over for the night? You don't want to exhaust yourself driving all the way to Sixton without any rest. And Toby, you'll need to rest, as well."

"Don't worry about me, Princess," Toby said.

Mr. Samlett shook his head vigorously. "No, no, no, Your Royal Highness. We're not tired. No, we're not tired at all. We'll ride until the dawn comes up. And then we'll eat a little something and ride some more."

"If you're sure," Ari said. She settled back on her heels. "Basil? Dill? Find a comfortable spot. Lori? You can cover yourself with that quilt."

"And you, Your Royal Highness, you get some sleep, too," Basil said in a kindly way. "I'll sit up front with Samlett, for a while."

Ari settled into a corner of the cart and pulled the extra quilt over her shoulders. She fell asleep.

And as she slept, she dreamed.

Arrrr-iiii-aaaannnna, a cold voice breathed in her ear.

Princessss, hissed another.

She woke with a start. The lanterns were out.

Up front, Toby jogged steadily on. Mr. Samlett held the reins in one hand, but his head was slumped forward on his chest. Ari heard the faint echo of a snore. Basil and Dill were intertwined on her lap. Sometime during the night, Lincoln had jumped into the cart. He slept at her side.

Lori slept with her mouth open.

Ari pushed herself upright and looked over the edge of the cart. Chase walked steadily beside it, his head low, his eyes abstracted. He looked into Ari's eyes as her head appeared over the side.

Do not speak, he thought at her.

What is it? Ari thought.

Do you hear it? Do you feel it?

Ari listened. Yes. There it was.

The cold sound of the snake. Ari shuddered. Chase arched his great neck over her and blew softly on her cheek. *Sleep, milady. It will not approach us this night. I will see to that.*

Ari slumped back into the cart and put her face in her hands. The last line of the Prophecy echoed in her brain.

Three of Six shall not return.

Linc, Chase, Basil, Dill, Lori. And she, Ari, herself. Six of them set out on an impossible journey. The Six referred to in the Old Mare's Prophecy.

Three of Six shall not return.

She was so tired! The way seemed so long! The task ahead of her was so hard!

Three of Six shall not return.

84

Linc and Lori were to pass through the Valley of Fear and go home, to Glacier River Farm.

Three of Six . . .

What if the Old Mare of the Mountain was wrong?

What if death lay ahead for all of them?

. . . shall not return.

11

"**I** will show you what I saw in the Valley of Fear,"
Dill said. They had stopped for a breakfast of wheat
cakes, honey, and fruit, near a tiny roadside market
about thirty miles outside of Sixton. It was early; dew
was still on the grass and the morning haze had not
yet been burned from the sky. Cultivated fields of
oats and sweet alfalfa spread to the east and west. A
few of the neighboring farmers were already in the
fields, hoeing the weeds and clearing the cropland
of those rocks and branches that had escaped the
spring harrowing. Two women sat under a gaily
striped canopy at the side of the road, selling sweet
milk, butter, cheese, and early summer berries. A
third sold bread and muffins from a rough shed.
They glanced at the cart once or twice, and raised
their hands in greeting. Ari wished she had money
to buy baked goods. The smell of the muffins was
delicious, even at a distance.

Dill sat on her haunches in the middle of the cart, bushy tail curled around her feet. Her pointed nose quivered with tension. "So you want to know about the Valley of Fear, Your Royal Highness," she said. "If you could spread some fine dirt on the floor, I can draw a map for you."

Ari jumped out of the cart and scooped up a handful of grit from the side of the road. She got back in and spread it in a thin layer in front of the vixen. She sat down with Lincoln on one side and Lori on the other. Toby, Mr. Samlett, and Chase stood outside the cart and peered over the side.

"The Valley lies on the northernmost shore of the Sixth Sea." Dill placed her paw carefully at the edge of the dirt, making a round spot. "From the shore, you take the Trail of Tears to the top of Demonview — a mountainous hill where it never stops snowing." She drew a thin line from the round spot to the middle of the dirt patch. "Then, it's down, down, down. The lower you go, the hotter it gets. You reach the Fiery Field. This is a terrible place, worse than the snows of Demonview. And there is . . ." Her voice dropped away. She shuddered. "The Fiery Field is patrolled by the shadow herd."

"The shadow herd?" Lori cleared her throat. "What is that?"

"Black unicorns. Black." Dill's voice was a mere thread. "With fiery eyes and horns like molten spears. The sand where they walk is black and hot. All around them, there are holes with fire."

"Lava bed," Lori said unexpectedly. At Ari's startled look she explained, "Sounds like there's a volcano around there somewhere."

"There is a waterfall of fire," Dill said. As soon as they were past the subject of the shadow unicorns, her courage seemed to have returned. "I don't know what a vol-can-oh is. Anyhow, you humans will have to walk this path without shoes."

"Without shoes?!" Lori said.

"There's a cooler path through the middle. Not much cooler, but cool enough so that you won't burn up if you step on it. You won't be able to feel the difference unless you have bare feet."

"You'll burn up if you step on the hotter part!" Lori said.

Dill nodded. Like Basil's, her mask surrounded her eyes and covered the top of her forehead. It made it harder to read her expression. "You get past the Fiery Field and you have to travel carefully around the Pit."

"The Pit?" Ari asked. "What's in the Pit?"

Dill didn't say anything for a moment. Basil, who was curled next to her, put a protective paw on her back. "She'll tell you what she can tell you."

"We go around the Pit," Ari said in an encouraging way. "And then?"

"You'll see it then. Castle Entia. And we just . . ." Dill took a deep breath. "We just walk in the front door."

"We just walk in?" Ari said. "Aren't there guards?"

"There's plenty of guards — if you can call those evil, twisted beings guards — to sneak past when we're in the Valley itself. But no, not at Castle Entia itself." Dill shook her head. "*He* doesn't need them at the Castle. Why should he? No one goes to Castle Entia unless they're summoned. It's not the kind of place that you hang around for fun. Half the time, the Shifter himself isn't even there."

"Atalanta said she and the Celestial Valley unicorns would create a diversion," Ari said. "So the Shifter won't be there, I hope."

Nobody said anything for a moment. Everyone was wondering what would happen if the diversion didn't work.

Dill broke the silence. "So. The Dreamspeaker is supposed to create a diversion, so that the Shifter and most of his army are going to be off chasing the Celestial unicorns. So *he* won't even be at home. And the Shifter won't leave guards when he's not there because it's worth your life to take anything that belongs to him." Dill shuddered. "You'll see what happens to thieves when we pass by the Pit. Who'd be crazy enough to ask for that kind of punishment?"

"We are," Lincoln said wryly. "If you ask me, it's hopeless. We're supposed to sneak past the monsters, ghouls, and shadow unicorns that live in the Valley of Fear, walk into the Castle Entia as nice as you please, and walk out again with the Royal Scepter? I can believe that the Shifter's subjects are so afraid of him that he doesn't need guards. But I can't believe that there isn't some hidden trap, just waiting for us."

"We'll be disguised as soldiers," Ari said, her voice much more hopeful than she felt. "And we don't really have a choice about how to get in. Maybe there's a back way."

Lori stood up, rocking the cart back and forth. She put her foot on the dirt map and rubbed it into nothingness. "Come on. Let's get this over with."

They left the peace and quiet of the roadside market and rode on into Sixton. They came to the outskirts of the town in the late afternoon. Great white seabirds soared high in the sky. Before they saw the houses and shops of the village, they smelled the sea. The salty air was soft and warm.

Sixton was a bustling, thriving town. "Everyone here's a fisherman," Toby said over his shoulder as he pulled the cart down the cobblestone streets. "They pretty much stayed out of the Shifter's war last year. They're too far from the Palace at Luckon to care much about government affairs one way or the other. But they're mostly loyal to the Crown."

He trotted briskly through the busy streets, and said no more.

Ari couldn't remember if she'd ever been in Sixton, and she looked around curiously. The whole town smelled of fresh fish. There seemed to be a fish shop on every corner — servants of the great houses brought carts and wagons from all over to buy Sixton's produce. Ari saw a wagon with the blue-and-yellow crest of the House of Harton and servants wearing the red livery of the House of Finglass. Her heart beat a little faster. If she could remember two of the seven Great Houses of Balinor, perhaps her memory was finally returning!

Chase drew attention, even though his coat had been dulled with grease and the ruby at the base of his horn painted over. It was the way he carried himself, Ari noticed with a sense of pride. Head held high, neck arched, there was majesty in every stride he took. Chase crowded close to Samlett's cart, and bent his great head to her. "You're smiling, milady."

"Do you see those men in the blue-and-yellow vests? And the two women in red? I remember which Houses they're from, Chase. And I don't even have the Scepter yet. Do you think I'll remember more and more as time goes on — without the Scepter?"

"Perhaps."

"It's just . . ." She was quiet for a moment, thinking. "What if we fail? What if we don't get the Scepter back? What if something goes wrong? I'm not afraid of the danger, you know," she said softly. "Well, maybe a little. But I am afraid to come back without the Scepter. If I could remember everything about my past all on my own, maybe there'd be a different way to find my parents and my brothers. If only so much didn't depend on me!"

Chase's muzzle briefly brushed her hair. "We are in this together, milady. If we fail — and I do not think we shall, not while I have breath in my body — we will find another way."

"Heads up," Toby called. "We're headed down to the wharf!" He made a sharp right, and they descended into the port of Sixton itself.

Sixton was located at the shore of a natural harbor. The sea took Ari's breath away. It stretched before her — calm, deep, an intense turquoise. Seagulls swooped and cried, their calls thin and cheerful in the late afternoon sun. The harbor itself formed an almost perfect semicircle, as if some giant long ago had chomped a large bite out of the land's flank.

More than a dozen wooden piers poked into the waters of the harbor. And the boats! There were all kinds of boats! Dinghies packed with nets and poles for deep-sea fishing, pleasure boats with silken sails, a racing sloop or two, and three large frigates. High-masted sails furled, they rocked in the gentle swell of the Sixth Sea.

"There it is," Toby said. "The *Dawnwalker.* She's the middle frigate. See it? The one painted deep green with the figurehead of the Dawn Princess on the prow."

Ari squinted. She could read the name on the ship's side. The letters were painted in gold: DAWNWALKER.

Toby came to a halt. "We'll leave you now, Your Royal Highness." He took a breath, as if to say something more. But then he merely nodded.

Ari, Lori, and Linc got out of the cart. Dill and Basil, after some minor squabbling about who should get out first, jumped out together and stood near Chase's hocks. Ari went up to Mr. Samlett on his perch and took his hand. "Thank you, Mr. Samlett." She raised herself on tiptoe and kissed his cheek. "We will see you soon, I hope."

The chubby landlord flushed bright pink. He bit his mustache to hide his pleasure in Ari's kiss. "We'll be waiting right here, Your Royal Highness, I say, right here. I have a cousin who's a lobsterman, lives a few miles up the village. Toby and I'll stay with him. We'll come to the wharf every morning to check for you."

"We shouldn't be gone too long," Ari said.

"And you won't see me again at all, Samlett," Lori said. "So, here's some pay for my room and board." She dug into the pocket of her velvet dress and pulled out a few small gold coins. Samlett accepted them with a nod of thanks.

"Where did you get the money, Lori?" Linc asked. A worried frown appeared between his dark brown eyes.

"Oh, I've got friends, same as you two," Lori said airily. " And Carmichaels always pay their bills."

"Thank you, miss," Mr. Samlett said. "I can't say as it's been a pleasure having you, I say, having you stay at the Inn. But I'm glad to get the bill settled."

Lori said, "Humph."

Ari took a deep breath. "Well!" She forced a smile. "We're off! See you in a few days, Mr. Samlett." She went to Toby and threw her arms around his neck.

"Stay safe," he grumbled, "and good luck."

With Lincoln on one side and Chase on the other, Ari set off for the *Dawnwalker.* She didn't look back. Lori mooched along behind, holding up the velvet skirt of her riding habit to avoid soiling it on the damp quay. Basil and Dill scurried ahead. They walked straight toward the deep green ship.

Behind them, a long, dark length slithered over the wooden walk.

12

Ari liked Captain Tredwell. He was tall, as broad as a barrel, and the part of his face visible over his chocolate-colored beard was tanned to leather. His eyes were gray; they looked as if they were used to staring into broad horizons. He was waiting to greet them as they walked up the gangplank to the *Dawnwalker*.

"Captain Nick Tredwell, at your service . . . milady." He swept off his captain's hat with a flourish and winked at Ari. "You'd be wishin' passage aboard the *Dawnwalker* for yourself and your companions?" He addressed Lori. Clearly, he had been warned of the group's need for disguise. Lori loved being treated like a wealthy lady. She stuck her chin in the air and nodded in an arrogant way. "Yes, Captain. I'd like the best cabin for myself. And my maid, too, I guess."

"And your destination, milady?"

Lori opened her mouth and then shut it.

"The north shore," Chase said quietly. "Near Demonview."

"Ah. Going to check on the ice-gatherers?" His voice slid easily over Lori's bewildered look. "I take it, milady, that you have sent members of your House ahead to gather ice to store the fish you'll be taking back home."

"Um. Well. Yes."

"Good! Good! A good mistress always checks on her servants. And Demonview is the only place in Balinor where you can obtain ice year-round."

"And thank goodness for that," Ari said, before Lori could jeopardize their disguise with questions. "Milady, I think you mentioned how tired you were after our trip. Wouldn't you like the captain to take us to our cabin?" She put her hand on Lori's back and gave her an unobtrusive shove. "Here! Let me help you cross the deck."

Lori shook Ari's hand off. "I can get there myself, thank you very much." She scowled at Ari. "Oh, Captain. The dog will need a place to sleep. I don't want him with us. I have . . . allergies. Maybe you can find a nice place for him in the open air. Like on that pile of rope over there."

Ari gave Lincoln a rueful look. He wagged his tail at her and grinned. "I'll stay with Chase, milady."

"Yes, we have a fine cabin for the unicorn," Captain Tredwell said. "Now, if you ladies will settle in, I have the sails to set. We want to catch the tide."

Ari didn't see much of the sailors' activity setting sail. She stayed in the cabin with Lori and unpacked their few belongings, "Because," as Lori pointed out, "it'll seem weird if I unpack for myself. I could get used to having a maid. Hah!" With a smirk, she settled into one of the hammocks that served as their beds.

Ari ignored her, and shook out the few clothes they'd brought with them. Her mind was full of the dangers ahead. She went over and over her mental map of the Valley of Fear. Demonview. The Fiery Field. The Pit. Castle Entia.

Three of Six shall not return.

Ari curled herself into a corner of the cabin and dozed. Nightmarish images floated in her mind.

Princess. She didn't want to be a Princess. Oh, if only things had been different!

She shook herself fully awake when one of the crew tapped on the cabin door and told them dinner was ready. She followed Lori outside. The sails were full and the wind brisk. The air had a clean, cold scent. The *Dawnwalker* forged steadily across the sea.

Ari looked up. Clouds rode high over the

water, obscuring the stars, hiding the fact that there was no moon.

Perhaps the Dreamspeaker was watching them from the pool in the Celestial Valley! Ari raised her hand and waved, then crossed the deck to the captain's cabin, where dinner waited.

13

Atalanta stood motionless at the edge of the Watching Pool. She was alone. Some distance away, the unicorns of the Celestial Valley waited for her. The image of Arianna on the deck of the *Dawnwalker* faded into the waters of the pool.

It was almost time. Tomorrow, as the sun rose over Demonview, the Dreamspeaker would lead an army of Celestial unicorns to Balinor, where they would challenge the Palace where the Shifter reigned. They wouldn't fight. They would race through the Forest of Ardit, the Shifter in hot pursuit.

"Are you sure that he will only follow us?" Numinor had asked. "May we not be prepared to fight?"

Atalanta had agreed. They would fight if they had to. She raised her crystal horn. She closed her eyes. Her silvery mane flowed over her withers.

"I call on the deep magic," she said, so softly

that only the One Who Rules could hear. "Transform me. Change me. For the sake of us all."

The waters of the pool churned. The waves sprayed high. A fine mist floated in the air. The mist whirled, took shape, then settled over the Dreamspeaker like a bridal veil, as fine as a spiderweb.

The net floated onto her horn, passed over her violet eyes, hid her completely. She grew in size. Her body darkened to a fiery purple. Her silver mane grew longer, thicker, swinging from her neck with a metallic clang. Her eyes burned with a fierce indigo flame.

The waters in the Watching Pool calmed. The mist drifted away. The unicorn called the Dreamspeaker no longer stood at the edge of the pool. A warrior unicorn stood there instead, chest and withers gleaming with chain mail, hindquarters covered with hammered silver shields. Her crystal horn was a diamond sword, flaming at the tip.

Atalanta took two steps and reared. She trumpeted a war cry to the sky. In the distance, Numinor answered, and with him, the call of the stallions of the Celestial herd. Atalanta leaned over and gazed at herself in the water. She shuddered at the sight of her own warlike image.

She *would* maintain it. If it took all of her strength and personal magic to do it!

"Oh, yes, Numinor," she said. "We are ready for the Shifter now!"

14

Arianna slept heavily that night. She woke up early and lay in her hammock, listening to the slap of waves against the hull of the ship. Lori was sound asleep in the other hammock. Ari swung herself onto the floor and pulled on her boots. She was, she decided, tired of sleeping in her clothes. She wanted a hot bath, to wash her hair, to ride Chase — anything rather than face what was coming.

She packed up her few belongings in her saddlebags. The Star Bottle with the water from Atalanta's Grove was at the top. She held it in her hand. It made her feel safer, closer to the Dreamspeaker and the faraway meadows of the Celestial Valley. On impulse, she tucked it into her leather vest. And Dr. Bohnes's red leather bag: She'd carry that with her, too. The old vet's words came back to her: *"Use it when there's no way out!"*

Ari let herself quietly out of the cabin. The dawn was misty and the whole world seemed veiled in low gray clouds. The sailors on deck looked at her, but didn't speak. Chase was standing at the prow of the *Dawnwalker*, his long mane blowing in the ocean spray. Lincoln stood next to him. Ari went to Chase and leaned against his warmth. Linc wagged his tail at them, and she caressed the white snip on his nose.

"Demonview," the unicorn said. He nodded, pointing his horn. "Off to starboard."

"There's snow on the top of the mountain," Lincoln said.

Ari forced herself to look. Demonview reared its jagged peak in front of them. It was close. The mountain's icy peak was a sullen white, now visible, now hidden as the wind pushed the clouds along.

Everything seemed frozen in this early light — all but the figure of a giant blackbird, riding the currents of air high above the ship. Ari glanced up at it. The bird circled the ship. She could just see its curved beak. She caught a glimpse of its dull black eye. There was something about that eye. Had she seen it somewhere before?

Suddenly, the bird swiveled its head around, as if receiving a far-off call. It screeched, a long, dying cry that made the hair on the back of Ari's neck prickle. Then it turned around and headed south, its powerful wings thrusting it forward at an amazing speed.

The unicorns of the Celestial Valley are advancing on Castle Entia, said a voice in Ari's mind. *The Shifter has already seen us. Soon the diversion will begin. It is time for you to go forward. Move swiftly through the Fiery Field, my child. But be careful. If you fail, all is lost.*

Atalanta! Somehow the Dreamspeaker talked to Ari the same way Chase talked to her — through her mind. But it was more than talk. It was a vision.

Ari could see the Celestial unicorns — hundreds and hundreds of them — marching on Castle Entia under the white banner of peace.

Numinor led the march. Rednal of the red band trotted beside him. Cinched to Rednal's flank was the tall white banner of peace. Numinor stopped on the hill overlooking the castle, and the Celestial unicorns gathered behind him.

"We come in peace, under a white flag!" Numinor called. "I, Numinor, the Golden One, Herd Leader of the Celestial Valley unicorns, shall speak to Lord Entia!"

A black unicorn trotted out of the castle, his red eyes shining with hatred. "What is your business here?" he sneered.

Behind him, more coal-black unicorns slipped silently out of the castle and into the dismal forest. Soon Numinor and his gallant band would be surrounded.

"My business is with your lord," Numinor stated proudly. "It is time we talked of peace, not war."

Ari cried out to Atalanta, *The Shifter has sent out his legions to surround Numinor and the Celestial unicorns. You must warn him before it's too late!*

Atalanta answered, *We expected this, Arianna. We knew the Shifter would not allow us to come and go in peace. Although we are not ready to fight a war, we can lead a merry chase. And we will fight if we have to!*

The evil unicorns leaped upon the rainbow herd. Numinor and the Celestial unicorns split up and galloped north, south, east, and west. The shadow unicorns were momentarily confused. It was the delay that Numinor and his troops had hoped would occur.

The shadow unicorns gave chase, but Ari could see that they were divided, running this way and that. They no longer held the advantage of surprise or superior position. The Celestial unicorns were faster, stronger, smarter. Evil and the lust for power had a way of corrupting the body and the mind.

Then, out of the castle flew the Shifter himself — this time transformed into the shape of a black dragon. His body was thick with muscle. His long wings sprang from his shoulders, stretched out like those of a gigantic wasp. His iron hooves grew grossly large. He had not one horn on his head but two, one behind each ear, curling up above his head in a huge ram's arc.

Where the Shifter's eyes and mouth should have been, there were exploding pockets of fire. Buried in the flames were black stars reaching out from the depths of dying galaxies.

Ari buckled at the knees. Was this what the Shifter truly looked like? Was it another terrible disguise? The vision faded. Ari felt Sunchaser lean against her body to support her.

"What is it, Princess?" he demanded. "What's wrong?"

"Nothing, Chase, I'm fine. Atalanta sent me a vision. Numinor and the Celestial unicorns have cleared the way for us."

You must go now, Arianna! said Atalanta. *We don't know how long we will be able to keep the Shifter and his legions away from the castle. We're all counting on you. Good luck!*

Yes, everyone was counting on her, Arianna, the Royal Princess. She trembled with fear.

"Your Royal Highness?" Captain Tredwell's voice was close behind her.

Ari jumped, then turned to him. "I'm sorry, I'm just the lady's servant."

The captain smiled kindly. "I'm no fool, Princess. I know Royalty when I see it. You'll be going ashore in about half an hour. I'll have to anchor the ship beyond the reef. We'll take you in with the dinghy."

"Thank you, Captain," Ari said.

"Do you have something for my companion?" Chase asked. "And for the four others who travel with us?"

"I almost forgot!" Captain Tredwell exclaimed. "Yes, I do. Your old nurse, Eliane Bohnes, sent it to me some days ago. She asked me to keep it safe for you." He looked doubtful. "It's a large package, Your Royal Highness. Will you be able to carry it?"

The disguises! Ari had almost forgotten them herself.

"We'll take it from here, Captain," Chase said. "Lincoln, would you please call the others — Dill, Basil, and Lori?"

Lincoln trotted off. In short time, the Six assembled on deck, and Demonview loomed in front of them. Ari stared up at its icy peak and shivered, rubbing her arms.

To Ari, the next half hour sped by in seconds. The cabin boy brought them hot tea and wheat cakes. The *Dawnwalker's* anchor was lowered, and the dinghy put into the water. One of the deckhands attached a short plank to a network of ropes to make a seat. He winched the plank into position, then stood at attention, waiting for orders.

Lori, her hair uncombed and a frown on her face, looked crossly at the captain. "We're going to sit on that thing?"

Captain Tredwell nodded.

"How's he going to get into that little boat?" She jerked her thumb at Chase.

Chase's eyes narrowed in amusement. "I'll see you ashore," he said. And before Ari could stop him, he leaped into the air and over the *Dawnwalker*'s side into the ocean. He landed with a tremendous splash, then struck out for the shoreline, swimming strongly. The black paint covering his ruby jewel washed away, and the jewel shone in the gray air like a beacon.

Captain Tredwell's eyes widened. "I have heard that the Sunchaser had returned with you, Your Royal Highness. Is that . . ." He stopped himself midsentence. "I am forbidden to ask more. Forgive me." He bowed in front of Ari, his gray eyes lively. "We will wait here three days. Then I must return to Sixton."

Ari nodded. Suddenly, she felt very tired. The words of the Old Mare's Prophecy haunted her: *Three of Six shall not return.* "Very good, Captain. We will meet you here sooner than that, I hope. It will take a day to reach our destination, and a day to come back."

Captain Tredwell's clear gray eyes darkened. "Milady, you know what lies on the other side of Demonview."

"Yes, Captain."

"I do not know your quest, Princess Arianna. But I wish you well. Did they warn you? Do you know where the Shifter's territory begins? It is not safe to go past the line of ice-gatherers."

"I know all about it," Dill said bossily. "Just get us into that boat, Captain. Chase is practically on land, and we're standing here gabbing the time away."

Ari, Lori, and Linc took their places on the plank. Basil and Dill sat in Ari's lap. One of the sailors winched the plank to a position just over the dinghy. The sailor manning the oars reached up, and the five of them scrambled into the boat. He shipped the oars expertly and turned the boat in the water. He rowed steadily, not speaking. Ari watched the north shore come closer and closer.

The sailor beached the dinghy. He hopped out into the water and pulled the little boat up onto the sand. Chase stood there waiting for them, seawater dripping from his bronze coat. He glowed like a lantern in the gray light. Ari helped Basil and Dill onto the sand. Then she and Lincoln got out. Lori sat huddled on her seat, her face pinched with fear.

"Are you coming?" Ari asked.

Lori looked at the sky. It was empty, except for the clouds. She bit her lip, nodded, and got out. The sailor tugged at his cap in farewell, then rowed the dinghy away.

Ari looked up at the forbidding mountain of Demonview.

They were on their way to the Fiery Field and the dark home of the Shifter.

15

"This is a disguise?" Lori shrieked. "This is *disgusting!*" She looked down at herself. She and Ari were dressed as soldiers in the Shifter's army, and Ari had to admit Lori was right. They looked creepy. But it was almost impossible to tell who they really were. Humans in the Shifter's army dressed in black leather from head to foot. The uniform consisted of leather pants with metal knee and shin guards and a close-fitted leather jacket. A breastplate worked in leather and metal was wrapped over the front of the jacket. The weapons belts were heavy; both Lori and Ari had a mace, a short sword, and a wooden implement that looked a little like a slingshot.

"Catapult," Chase said. "There should be small iron balls to go with it."

Ari dug in the bag. There were a dozen iron balls, with places in the weapons belt to hold six each. But it was the helmet that provided the most protection. The leather skullcap fit tightly over the skull. A faceplate attached to it completely hid the wearer's face. Ari's chief problem was her hair. She coiled it on top of her head, and pulled the leather collar of the jacket over the back of her neck. She put the helmet on and presented herself to Chase. "What do you think?"

The great unicorn nodded his approval.

"Grim," Lincoln offered. "You look grim."

Dr. Bohnes had also provided helmets for Chase, Linc, and the two foxes. There was a container filled with a sticky, tarlike substance. Ari rubbed this over Chase's horn and the ruby jewel. Then she rubbed it over the rest of him. She'd dulled his coat with grease for the trip to Sixton, but it had been nothing like this. When she finished her work, Chase was completely black. His horn was an iron spear. His eyes glittered at her through the eye holes in the mask. A shiver went up Ari's spine.

She and Lori covered the foxes and the dog with sticky dye, then fitted them with helmets. They looked at one another. The disguises were perfect. Ari had a cover story ready if they were stopped by any of the Shifter's subjects: They were a scouting party, out to search for deserters.

"Well," Lori said, "I guess we're ready."

"Wait." Ari took the Star Bottle and Dr. Bohnes's leather bag out of her vest and tucked them in her weapons belt. Then Lincoln dug a hole

in the sandy shore, and Ari put their discarded belongings in it.

"Okay." Ari took a deep breath. "Now."

They marched across the sandy beach to the
foot of Demonview and began to climb. The path
was rocky, with an almost vertical slope. The dog
and foxes had the easiest time of it, scrambling over
stones with their feet splayed, using their claws to
grip the rocky terrain. Chase took the mountain in
great leaps, launching himself into the air and land-
ing with delicate precision in just the right spots.

Ari and Lori sweated their way up, crawling
along on all fours.

The higher they went, the colder it got.
Clouds swirled about them, obscuring the way. They
passed an occasional party of ice-gatherers, chip-
ping away at chunks of ice, loading it in baskets to
carry on down the mountain to be shipped back
to Balinor. The ice-gatherers straightened up and
turned their backs when the Six passed them. Lincoln put his muzzle to the air and sniffed. "They are
afraid," he said. "There is nothing quite like the smell
of fear."

"The disguises are working well," Dill said.
"Let's hope the folks on the other side of this ratty
mountain believe it, too."

The last yards to the top were the worst.
Snow swirled around them, a cold dense blanket. It
was hard to see more than a few feet in front of

them. Ari organized her companions into a line and ran a rope among them, Chase at the head, Lori after him, with herself at the end. If they lost sight of one another in this thick blizzard, they might never find one another again.

They struggled on. The cold numbed their feet and bit fiercely at their cheeks and ears. Lincoln's fur was matted with snow. Dill was white with it. Only Chase appeared unaffected, his great body steaming in the frigid air.

Ari slipped, slid, and crawled her way up, up, up. Her fingers reached out, clutching the rope, and she stumbled to her feet.

They were at the top!

Chase stood next to her, looking down. Dill and Basil sat down in the snow and bit the ice balls from their paws. Lincoln pressed close to Ari's side. Lori stood off by herself, arms wrapped around her body, shivering.

Ari gazed down at the Valley of Fear.

There was no snow on this, the Shifter's side of Demonview. The mountain's barren sides plunged to a vast, black expanse of sand. Steam drifted up from fire-filled holes pocking the landscape. A faint odor of rotten eggs reached Ari. *Sulfur,* she thought.

The Fiery Field was swollen with hummocks of sand and black granite. Black dots moved in clusters on it, like maggots on a log. Work parties? Soldiers? There weren't many. Ari thought about the message Atalanta had sent her: Even now, the bulk of the Shifter's army was chasing the Celestial unicorns through the Forest of Ardit.

She hoped.

The horizon of the Valley of Fear was filled with dense, oily smoke. It coiled around itself like a huge, undulating snake. Through the coils, Ari could just glimpse a sprawling building. Two turrets stood on either end. The middle had a steep roof. It was hard to tell in the shifting smoke, but it seemed that an iron fence circled the massive castle.

Castle Entia. At least a day's walk away.

Take no food or water, Atalanta had said.

It was going to be a thirsty hike.

Without a word to one another, they began the trek down the desolate sides of Demonview. The cold air grew warm, then hot. Sweat trickled down Ari's back and made great patches on Chase's sides. They scrambled through thorny brush that sliced through Ari's leather jacket. She bit her lip and kept on.

They reached the bottom of the mountain after a nightmare of harsh gravel and painful scratches.

"Stop here," Dill said in a low voice.

Ari halted and stretched her aching muscles. She had an urgent desire to rip off her helmet and take in great gulps of air. A low sobbing made her rigid with fear; she turned. Lori sat on a rough piece of lava rock, her helmet on her knee. Her blond hair

113

tumbled over her shoulders. Her face was streaked with dirt.

"Put your helmet back on, Lori," Ari said softly.

"I can't! I'm so *hot!*"

"It's going to get hotter," Dill said. "Put your helmet back on and take off your boots."

"I can't!"

"Then," Dill said brutally, "we'll leave you here."

"You wouldn't! You couldn't!"

Dill looked at Ari, a question in her golden eyes. Ari shook her head. "We're all in this together. I won't leave any of you. But we have to go on, Lori. We can't stop now. This is the only way you'll get home to see your father."

"All right!" Lori jammed her helmet on her head and tore off her boots. Ari pulled her own boots off and tucked them under her arm.

"Follow me!" Dill said. "Walk carefully. The fire shifts, so a spot where I'm able to step can be cool one minute and boiling the next. Whatever you do — *don't stop!*"

Ari placed one foot lightly in front of the other, drawing back instantly when she came close to the searing heat. Lori's screams, muffled by the helmet, told her Lori wasn't as careful. Ari made them all stop, while she explained again how to get through the terrible ashes.

"I can't do it!" Lori cried. "I can't!"

"Then I will carry you," Chase said.

"Not a good idea." Dill squeezed her eyes shut and opened them wide. "You can't be as agile with someone on your back. The weight will slow you down. You'll burn your hooves, Chase."

"Give her a leg up," Chase commanded.

"Your Royal Highness!" Dill said indignantly. "Are you going to allow this?"

"We have to," Ari said. "I'll say it as many times as I have to say it: We're all in this together. Here, Lori. Put your foot in my hands." Ari positioned herself carefully next to Chase. This near to the great unicorn, she could smell singed hair and hooves. She swallowed her own tears. Lori put her right foot clumsily in Ari's cupped hands and scrambled on top of Chase. She clung there, crying.

They started again. Ari followed the tip of Dill's tail, stepping where the fox stepped. The stench of burning lava seemed to choke and gag everyone.

The path wound on and on. Ari's movements grew automatic: touch; draw back; touch again; step. She imagined hideous faces in the coals beneath her feet — faces with slitted eyes and protruding tongues. She tried to breath shallowly.

"Princess!"

Dill's voice, close to her ear.

"Your Royal Princess!"

Ari snapped awake.

"We're out!" The little vixen hissed triumph-antly. "Now all we have to do is get by the Pit!"

Ari pulled herself together. She breathed deeply. The Fiery Field was behind them. Ahead was sand and gravel. No trees. No shade. No water. But at least no burning heat. Ari ran her hands carefully over Chase, checking for burns and singe marks. He refused to lift his hooves for her inspection. She bit her lip. She knew he was burned. She made Lori get down and put her boots back on. She pulled her own boots over her seared feet, biting back a shout of pain. She checked Lincoln over, who suffered more from smoke inhalation than burns, and looked at the foxes' paws. Everyone had suffered burns, but none of the burns looked worse than blisters.

"Okay." Ari nodded to Dill. "Now the Pit."

"Form a single file. Don't stop," Dill warned. "Keep on going. No matter what you see."

They heard the Pit before they saw it. The tramp of iron hooves on stone, shouts, groans, the crack of a whip. It lay to the right of the stony path. Ari kept her eyes lowered. Dill led the way, Chase right behind her. Ari was behind Chase. She saw Chase's hindquarters bunch, as if he were going to leap. She saw his horn lower, as if he were going to fight. She heard Dill's cautionary hiss, and thought at him, *Steady, Chase, steady!*

And then she saw it — the Pit. Her own hand

darted toward the knife in her weapons belt. She must free them! The poor slaves!

The Pit was a great hole gouged in the middle of the Valley of Fear. A narrow roadway spiraled to its smoldering depths. Dozens of animals worked the Pit, harnessed by the neck to stone collars. The shadow unicorns, those that Ari had seen when she first came to Balinor, surrounded the lip of the Pit, iron horns ready to spear any of the animals who tried to run away. Their red eyes gleamed, and their black coats shone.

The Six walked past in silence. Ari saw the wounds and scars the cruel collars made in the necks of the animals trapped there.

And suddenly, she remembered. The thin red scar around Dill's neck! The vixen had been here, a slave in the Valley of Fear, and had somehow escaped! So *that's* why she knew how to draw the map.

Ari made a vow. She would come back. She would get the Scepter and come back. One day she would free the poor slaves here!

"Brother!" A unicorn, larger than the others, shouted at Chase. "Where are you bound?"

Chase came to a halt. Ari went to his side, laid a calming hand on his neck. She watched the shadow unicorn gallop toward them, her heart in her throat. Close up, he would see through Chase's disguise.

"Come no nearer, brother," she said loudly. "We carry disease."

The shadow unicorn came to a halt. He squinted his red eyes at them. "You what?"

"A vomiting illness," Ari said, inventing as she went along. "With fever. It will go through the herd like a man with a scythe in a wheat field."

"Huh," the shadow unicorn said. He walked two strides toward them, head cocked to one side. His iron horn gleamed wickedly sharp. Two other shadow unicorns eyed the Six suspiciously. "I've never heard of such a thing," the first one said. "Who are you, anyway? I don't recognize the horn markings." The two other shadow unicorns started to argue about the horn markings. Horn markings? From the argument, Ari gathered that the squads of shadow unicorns were marked differently. There were no markings at all on Chase's horn. Ari bit her lip. Her hand went to her weapons belt. She fumbled for her catapult. That was the weapon to use. It might give them time to run.

Instead, her hand fell on the bit of soap she carried for washing her face.

Soap! She almost screamed with frustration. What was she supposed to do with soap? Wash the arguing unicorn's mouth out with soap?

Soap!

"Chase! Chew on this!" she hissed. She slipped the soap into his mouth. He worked it around with his lips. Foam dripped down his muzzle.

"You see, brothers!" Ari called. She pointed at Chase. "We think he has the summer madness! Rabies!"

Even the shadow unicorns were afraid of rabies. The summer madness struck without warning, sending its victims mad with fear and thirst.

"Go on!" the biggest one shouted. "Get out of here!"

Chase nudged Ari forward. She forced herself to walk slowly, slowly, until the Pit was far behind them all.

They stopped. The sun beat down mercilessly. Ari was so thirsty her tongue was swollen. Lincoln panted dreadfully in the heat.

"I can't go on," Lori panted. "I've got to have water!"

"Atalanta said not to carry anything into the Valley," Ari said. Her tongue was so thick with thirst she could hardly speak. "Everything here is poison, I guess."

"Well, I can't go on," Lori said. Her voice was so faint Ari could hardly hear her. "I can't."

"When there's no way out," Dr. Bohnes had said. *"Use it when there's no way out!"* And — *"My magic is for small things."*

Ari fumbled for the leather bag. She drew it from her tunic and opened it with shaking fingers. She looked inside.

There was only a small dish and a rock. Ari could have screamed with disappointment. Instead, she shook the little dish onto the ground and laid the pebble beside it. She stared at the dish — then, the half-forgotten legend of the unicorn's horn came back to her. "Chase," she croaked, water-starved. "Chase . . ." She waved one hand at the dish.

Chase nodded. Slowly, he walked up to her and slowly lowered his horn until the tip touched the small dish. For a moment, nothing happened. Then, with a pale blue shimmer, a pool of water formed at the bottom of the bowl!

Lori leaped on it with a shriek and gulped it down.

"There, now!" Dill hissed angrily. "How dare you, you little rat! That should have been for Her Royal Highness."

"It doesn't matter," Ari said softly. "She had the most need."

"We all have need," Chase said gravely. "Put the bowl back on the ground, Lori."

Sullenly, Lori set the dish back on the hot ash. Chase touched it again: The dish filled up. Ari picked the bowl up and offered it to Dill. To her relief, Dr. Bohnes's magic worked every time Chase touched his horn to the bowl, and at last, everyone had a cooling drink. Then Chase cocked his eye at the pebble with a mischievous look. "Shall I?" Without waiting for an answer, he lowered his horn. The rock transformed itself into bread! Ari divided the pieces carefully, making sure that everyone got an equal share, saving her own hunger for last.

Finally, they were all fed. They sat on the ground for a moment, silent, feeling their strength return.

"How far now?" Ari asked.

"Not far at all." Dill pointed with her slim muzzle. "Look ahead. Look ahead."

Ari raised her eyes. There it was, dark and forbidding. The two turrets on either side. The high, pointed roof in the middle.

Castle Entia. The home of the Shifter.

16

They walked right through the front gates and into the castle. They saw no one and heard nothing. The interior was dark, huge, and quiet. The floor was dark polished stone. The walls soared to unimaginable heights. Ari couldn't see the ceiling. She would not have guessed the ceiling was that high. Perhaps it was some dark magic, which made the inside seem greater than the outside.

Lincoln's claws went tick-tick on the stone floor. Chase stood like a statue, ears forward, head up.

"Where do we look?" Lori's voice echoed eerily in the huge space.

"Be *quiet*!" Dill hissed.

"I'm taking this *helmet* off," Lori said crossly. "I'm so hot, I can't stand it! And I'm thirsty again." She pulled it off her head.

Lincoln rounded on her ferociously. "If you don't shut up, I will bite you!" he snarled. "The place looks empty, but the last thing we need is to be discovered by any of those black unicorns."

"Well, you don't have to worry," Lori said confidently. "We're supposed to meet someone here."

"What?" Ari pulled her own helmet off. It was hard enough to see in the dark; it was even harder with the helmet on. "Meet who?"

"I didn't think much of this plan, you know." Lori set her helmet on the floor and ran her hands through her hair. "Gosh, I'm sweaty. Anyway, I heard that after you got into this place, it wasn't so bad. Especially since this Shifter guy isn't here."

"Who told you that?" Chase demanded sharply.

"I did." Lady Kylie glided toward them. Ari looked at her, bewildered. Where did she come from?

"You must be so tired. And so thirsty!" Lady Kylie said. She smiled smoothly. "Come and have something cold to drink. And a bit of food."

"I don't think so," Lincoln muttered. "Besides, we're full."

"Lori's right, you know. It's safe here, at least for now. *He* is gone. Away from . . ." Kylie bit her words off. She strained forward, peering into the gloom. Lady Kylie's flat black eyes glittered, elongated. The pupils narrowed into a snakelike slit. She slithered up to Ari and grabbed her chin in one cold, scaly hand. "So you are here for a reason, Princess?"

"I am on a journey," Ari said calmly. "And your master is not at home, is he, Lady Kylie?"

"Lori betrayed us!" Dill cried. "I told you she looks like that ferret!"

"You shut up!" Lori screeched furiously. "I haven't betrayed anybody. Lady Kylie said this would be a hard trip and it was. She said if we made it to the castle safely, she'd be here to help us get that stupid Scepter so I can go home! I haven't betrayed anyone!"

"You fool!" Chase roared. "Don't you know who Kylie is?!"

Lori looked uncomfortable. "She's the sister of Lord Lexan," she said. "And she's my friend."

Dill snorted. "Hah! She's a lot of things, Lori. Like the Shifter, she changes herself to suit the occasion. In Balinor, sure, she's Lord Lexan's sister. And she was the Queen's best friend. But she sold out, didn't you, Kylie? Sold out for power. She betrayed the Queen and the King. And in return, the Shifter gave her the Power of the Snake!"

Kylie laughed. A low, ugly, snakelike laugh. Her tongue flicked in and out of her mouth. It was red and forked—a serpent's tongue.

"The Power of the Snake?" Lori sounded scared.

Dill squeezed her yellow eyes open and shut.

"Nasty kind of magic, if you ask me. She can change into a snake as quick as you please. And she has all the nastiness of those reptiles, too. Sneaky, crawly, lethal things. And all so she could swank around to be Second-in-Command of the Shifter's army."

"Bite your tongue," Kylie purred. She writhed, and the dim light played across her thin lips. She smiled evilly at Chase. "This what you're after, isn't it, my pet? My Sunchaser." She held up her right hand. She was holding a short, beautifully carved staff. It glimmered briefly with a warm, rosy color. Rosewood inlaid with lapis lazuli.

The Royal Scepter.

So Atalanta had been right. They would find the Royal Scepter near one of the Shifter's greatest victories. And this victory had been to make Kylie turn traitor!

Kylie laid it with great care at her feet. Its glimmering light went out.

"Well!" Lady Kylie began to sway back and forth. Her body grew slimmer, longer. Her robes merged with her body and turned into scales. She writhed there, the snake. The Shifter's counselor.

Lori screamed.

"And I have you now, don't I? He will be so pleassssed. My masssster!" She stretched to an enormous height. Darkness swirled around her. Chase reared and trumpeted a challenge, then lowered his horn, prepared to charge. With a shriek, the snake writhed and dropped, coiling around Lori, who was so terrified she couldn't even scream. Ari reached for her knife, determined to hack away at those lethal coils.

"Don't move,"Kylie hissed. She tightened her coils. Lori gasped, a faint, pitiful sound that went straight to Ari's heart. She put her sword back into her weapons belt.

The bottle, Chase thought at Ari. *Princess.The Star Bottle!*

Ari remembered the Dreamspeaker's words: *"Use it only when all is dark and there seems no hope."* Ari fumbled at her belt for the Star Bottle.

Kylie laughed. "Now you will come with me! I will imprisssson you until my masssster returnssss! And then, *then* we sssshallll sssseeee!"

Ari held the Star Bottle up. It flickered, dimmed in the huge hall. "Atalanta,"Ari said.

"Atalanta!" Chase cried.

"Atalanta!" Dill, Lincoln, and Basil shouted until the roof rang with their calls. The Star Bottle burst into light, brighter than the moon, more glorious than the stars. The snake shrieked in agony, flinging herself away from the brilliance. The light seemed to blind only the snake.

Lori fell free, scrambled to her feet, and ran to Ari. Lincoln sprang forward and grabbed the Scepter in his jaws. Dill and Basil rushed at the snake, one on each side, jaws snapping furiously. Chase reared and struck the stone floor with a mighty clanging sound that made the walls shiver and the air shake.

The snake hissed, spat, and twisted, trying to hide her eyes. But at each frantic turn the foxes were there, needlelike teeth flashing.

"I am not your slave anymore!" Dill cried. She ducked and bit and darted in again.

"For my mate!" Basil shouted. He sprang forward and sank his teeth into the snake's tail. They drove the snake before them, like dogs herding sheep, snapping and snarling. The snake hissed, whipping her tail, fangs bared.

But the foxes were quick and clever. They drove the snake down the hall and out of sight.

When they returned, Dill's eyes were peaceful. "Well," she said. She sat down and scratched herself heartily. Ari could see the thin scar around her neck. "Well," she said again. Basil sat beside her and licked her ears.

Lincoln trotted up to Ari, the Scepter in his jaws. He crouched down carefully and dropped it at her feet.

Ari tucked the Star Bottle in her weapons belt, bent over slowly, and picked up the Scepter. It felt — right — in her hands, like something she'd been born to carry. It belonged to her. She held it carefully, feeling the warmth of the wood as if it were a living thing.

Chase came up to her. Ari stroked his nose

with one hand. Then, she grabbed his mane in her left hand, and held the Scepter in her left. She sprang up from the floor and mounted his back.

This, too, felt right. She belonged here. She held the Scepter up. There was a unicorn's head at the top, carved in wood, traced with precious blue stone. The eyes gleamed at her with something of the clear wisdom of the Old Mare of the Mountain. The rosy glow around the Scepter deepened, engulfed both Chase and Ari in a cleansing wash of light.

The unicorn head spoke in a deep yet distant voice. *"Arianna. Arianna. You shall remember now."*

And Ari remembered.

Slowly, as if a sun flooded her being with the light of dawn. Dinner with her father and mother after a day by the seashore. Her brothers, Bren and Stally, playing a complicated game of hide-and-seek in the Palace gardens.

Chase and the magic they could do together. The healing touch of Sunchaser's horn, when they worked to heal sickness in the village. The long conversations with the animals in the Forest of Ardit, and the settlement of small arguments among them. And Lincoln, there was something about Lincoln that she needed to learn. And only the Scepter could help her. The Scepter could help her with all these things. There was much more to learn from the Scepter! She and Chase had been in training with it — a training which had been interrupted by the Great Betrayal. Yes, she could use the Scepter to rule — but she would need time to learn about its powers.

"Time," the unicorn's head said. "There is no time. The Shifter's army approaches. And you must leave this place."

The Sunchaser's coat became bronze again. The ruby jewel at the base of his horn glowed in answer to the Scepter's own color.

Ari jerked herself out of the dream. She looked at Chase, his face alight, her heart singing. She flung her arm around his neck. "Well," she said into his glossy neck. "I guess this was worth it, after all."

"Milady!" Dill's tones were urgent. "I think we'd better get out of here. Now!"

"I agree," Lincoln said. "We've been lucky so far. And I want our luck to hold."

Ari tapped Chase lightly with her heels. Holding the Scepter before her, the two proceeded out of Castle Entia. Lincoln, Basil, and Dill followed. Lori ran after them, her face still pale with shock.

Princess Arianna and the Sunchaser rode into the Valley of Fear.

"I remember," Arianna said aloud, with gladness. "I remember everything." Her mother, blond and slim. Her father, the King. Her beloved nurse, Bohnes, and the Palace they lived in before the Great Betrayal.

Where Chase and Ari walked, the dirt and

gravel of the Valley of Fear turned to healthy green grass. Thorn bushes burst into bloom. They walked, the six of them back to the Pit, the Royal Scepter held like a beacon before them.

Ari rode Chase to the edge of the Pit, and scribed a circle in the air with the Scepter. Wherever its light fell, the chains and shackles fell away from the prisoners, and the air was filled with shouts of joy. The shadow unicorns fled deeper into the Pit. The prisoners ran for freedom, crying their thanks to the Royal Princess.

Tears of joy came to Ari's eyes. She had promised to free the slaves from the Pit, and she had kept that promise. Perhaps there were some good things about being Princess, after all.

"Ari!" shouted Lincoln. "There's something wrong — it's Lori!"

"What has she done now?" asked Ari.

"She's gone into the Pit."

"Oh, no. She *couldn't* have."

Ari dismounted Chase and followed Lincoln.

"This way." Lincoln paced down to the Pit. Ari clutched the Scepter — she wasn't about to let it out of her hands now, after all that trouble! — and walked with Chase to the head of the road that wound down into the bowels of the huge hole.

"She went down there." Lincoln nodded. Ari leaned over the edge. She saw a small figure with a faint gleam of blond hair. She braced herself against

Chase and leaned further. "Lori? Lori! Come back! I —"

She heard the rasp of scales on rock too late. She whirled, one hand on Chase's mane.

The snake loomed, huge, menacing, jaws open wide to bite. Ari jerked back without thinking.

She fell. She fell over the edge of the Pit, and with a shout, Chase leaped after her. She fell endlessly into the black, Scepter in her hand, its light bobbing wildly. She hit something soft, bounced, rolled, and then — for a moment — all was a confused whirl of bronze unicorn, blond hair, her own feet, and a dizzying blinding light.

She fell on her back with a thump that knocked the breath from her and made her head swim. She lay still, remembering what her nurse Bohncsy had said: "Don't get up right after a fall, Your Royal Highness. Make sure all your bones are in place."

She wiggled her right hand. Yes, that was okay. Then her left. Then her toes. She sat up carefully. Blinked. She was in a familiar meadow. It was surrounded by white three-board fencing. A herd of horses grazed nearby.

Horses? There weren't any horses in Balinor!

Ari got to her feet. Chase was next to her, a confused expression in his eyes. Lori was sitting down, her head in her hands.

Milady! Chase thought at her. *Where are we?*

"Oh, dear," Ari said. She held the Scepter tightly. "Oh, *dear!*" She looked around. "We're back, Chase! We're right back where we started! Glacier River Farm! We've crossed the Gap!" She went over to Lori and helped her to her feet. "Well, Lori," she said. "You're home! Just as the Dreamspeaker promised."

Lori looked around in a dazed way. A huge smile spread across her face. "You're right!" she said, astonished. "I'm home! Oh, thank you, Ari. Thank you! After I was so awful about Lady Kylie. The thing is . . . she promised . . . I'm . . ."

"It's okay," Ari said quickly. Lori being apologetic was almost worse than Lori whining. "Let's not talk about it anymore, okay?"

Lori dusted the seat of her leather pants. "Gosh," she said. "I don't suppose you counted on being here, too?"

"No," Ari said ruefully. "But that's what the Prophecy said, come to think of it. Three shall not return to Balinor. At least, not right now." She looked at the Scepter. "Although I'm pretty sure I remember now how to get us back. I'll figure it out if I have enough time."

Lori nodded. "Well, that's good," she said. "But if you're going to be at Glacier River Farm for a bit, you're going to have to do something about his horn."

They stood and looked at Chase. He stood tall and proud among the horses, his horn black and gorgeous and very, very obvious.

132

"I mean," Lori said, "people will wonder!"

"So they will." Ari threw her arms around her unicorn. "But I'll figure that out, too. First, we're going to say hello to Ann and Frank. And then, Chase, it's back home to Balinor!"

About the Author

Mary Stanton loves adventure. She has lived in Japan, Hawaii, and all over the United States. She has held many different jobs, including singing in a nightclub, working for an advertising agency, and writing for a TV cartoon series. Mary lives on a farm in upstate New York with some of the horses who inspire her to write adventure stories like the UNICORNS OF BALINOR.